Cake

Cake

a novel by

D

The Armory
Brooklyn

This is a work of fiction. All names, characters, places, and incidents are the product of the author's imagination. Any resemblance to real events or persons, living or dead, is entirely coincidental.

Published by Akashic Books
©2008 D

ISBN-13: 978-1-933354-54-5
Library of Congress Control Number: 2007939599

First printing

The Armory
c/o Akashic Books
PO Box 1456
New York, NY 10009
info@akashicbooks.com
www.akashicbooks.com

JUN   2008

CONELY BRANCH

START

There's no time like the first time. Because it's the first time that you can never shake loose. You see the make-believe version of murder all the time. You cheer for that shit on the big screen. You can't wait for the point when the bad guy's soul evacuates its temple so that he can be judged from up above. But it ain't the same thing in the real world.

In real life, the aftermath is a walking daymare. You can still see her face: eyes swollen shut, teeth cracked and chipped, cuts and bruises and broken ribs. You see your hand extending with a pistol in its grip. You remember just how little effort it took to actually pull the trigger. It was the night that changed your life, a change that did nothing but bring more changes.

You can still feel the warmth of her mouth around your dick. You can still envision the way she made her titties jiggle as you came on them, white on caramel, your exchanges hidden from view by glass painted black. You remember the depth of her voice as she whispered what you paid her to say. You can't believe that they made her into the bloody mess you capped out.

But it wasn't like you did it in cold blood. The men all around you in that house had clear instructions. If you didn't pop her, they were going to pop you. Plain and simple. There was nothing you could do but the deed.

"Trustin' bitches is like trustin' junkies," Star used to say. He's been dead for weeks now, his nine lives having finally run out, not from a bullet but some head-on collision in Kingston. What he was doing there you'll never know. It turned up on your Google alert one morning. Another loose end tied. Chief and Will couldn't reach that far, or at least you don't think so.

If Death wants you he's going to take you, guaranteed.

You thought it was your turn on that night all those months ago. But it wasn't. You're still waiting though. You know the sound that other shoe will make when it hits the floor. That's why you pray every day. That's why the first thing you did when you got back to town was get a new tool, a Glock 19 fresh from the gun fair in Conyers.

It's like the Brady Bill never happened down here. You tell some redneck's girlfriend that you want to make a quiet sale. A few Benjamins later you've got a burner in a shopping bag and not a lick of paperwork to show for it. You keep it close—not close enough to catch a charge if some rib tip pats you down, but close enough that if you need to make a point you can get to it in time, wedged between the cover and the spare in the back of your ride.

The other bodies that came after her didn't carry the same weight on your soul. It had always been self-defense. And it had been God who made your bullets hit while others missed. You had just been a boy making deliveries. You hadn't lived by the sword until that night.

Six months have gone by like nothing. You don't know whether Will and Chief are alive or dead. You don't know if there's a warrant out on you, or if there were any witnesses to your deeds. You walked away with a quarter of a mil and an Amtrak ticket out of town. You slept like a baby all the way down. That was one of the last times you didn't expect to open your eyes and find a pistol in your face.

You still have this funny feeling that it ain't over, this sense that someone from your old life is still on your trail. It's harder to change your name in a post-9/11 world, harder to hide when the right people can get all kinds of info about you with the click of a button. You feel like there's this clock inside your soul counting down to the end of the line, and the only one who can stop it is the Man upstairs, if he so chooses. But that's a call he's never going to make for an asshole like you.

1.

"**W**atch this part right heah, nigga!"
You don't think Duronté has ever cleaned a real dish in his life. The whole place is full of napkins and plastic knives and forks, but he's got a .45 stripped into a thousand pieces on the coffee table, polishing every part as if it came out of his mama's womb.

He sucks on the roach in his left hand until it starts to burn his fingers. Then he tosses it into the ashtray on top of a pile of what looks like hundreds of others. There's a half-killed carton of shrimp fried rice on the edge of the coffee table. There's no way in hell he should be this skinny with as much as he eats. Those particular genes of his must come from the other side of the family.

The walls have wood paneling on them that probably got put in thirty years ago, back when it was stylistically *the shit*. There's a framed photograph of his mother, Mabel, a big woman with Duronté's name tattooed on her left breast. While most women get their tattoos in their teens and twenties, she got hers at thirty-six, right after he bought her a used car with money he'd put away after an extremely successful six months of selling 'dro to all the local wannabe high rollers, D-boys, and potheads who couldn't find a connect like his in all of the ATL. As it turned out, that connect was Duronté's old English teacher, who had been running a grow house out in Alpharetta for longer than either of you had been alive.

Your cousin, despite his success, makes a lot of mistakes. It's a three-man operation with no real muscle. His boy Meechie did three on an assault charge. That's his heavy hitter. If somebody put him to the test, that .45 on the table would be the best he'd have to offer up. And that ain't good. That really ain't good.

"C'mon, nigga," he barks again, his eyes still glued to the screen. "You gotta check this shit out."

You shouldn't be watching two guys fuck Ayana Angel on DVD, especially not with another man in the room. That's too many dicks in the same sitting for any straight dude. Him even asking you can be considered a violation of etiquette. But there's something about the way Ayana's tremendously round ass swings like a piece on a chain, the click of those suicidally high heels, that makes you say fuck it and plop down on the couch. You haven't had pussy since Brooklyn. You've been too scared, too worried that the life that 250 Gs built for you won't be enough.

"You know she live up in Buckhead, right?" he says, as if he's been plotting on finding the address. You can imagine him showing up at a porn star's front door in a wife beater, cornrows, and khakis, looking to get laid. Broads like her charge by the hour as a side business, a way to make up for the royalties she doesn't get paid from her bread-and-butter work.

You've been sleeping on this very couch for a week now. It's lumpy in the middle and reeks of old cigars and stale french fries. Your cousin's second mistake is that he deals right out of his own house. His crew takes the bulk of it to some satellite locations like the car wash he has a piece of on Old National and the ice cream truck that circles Piedmont Park in the summer. But if you want a brick, all you have to do is dial his traceable cell, make an appointment, and walk right up to the front door. It's a thief's wet dream. Luckily for you, this housing situation is only temporary.

There's a place on Palmetto, just a few blocks from here and your soon-to-be campus. Your name is on the deed. But the Hondurans won't be done with the renovations for another week or two. That's why you dug up your wild-ass third cousin after finding his mama's number in the file juvie services gave to you when you turned eighteen. You are their only living New York relative. But the real reason Duronté likes you is that you know how to act in the street, that you can point out the flaws in his operation, that you can help him to be more legit. You don't need to stay with him, but you want to. He is now the only familiar face in a world full of strangers. Some of the same blood runs through your veins. And for some reason that makes his couch more like home than almost any other bed you've slept on.

You told him about what you did for Star. You told him about the pile of bodies you left behind. From the look on his face you thought he was going to bust all over himself with excitement and admiration. And you used that to your advantage.

Truth be told, Duronté went to private school growing up. He just didn't have the grades to get into anywhere other than Georgia State. He takes, like, a class a semester so that Mabel will let him stay in the house rent free, the one she inherited from her mother while she was living it up in a marriage of convenience with some Polish guy in his fifties who couldn't get a visa because he had a criminal record back in the homeland. She's shopping at Saks Fifth Avenue while her baby boy sells sacks in the SWATS. That shit is kind of ironic when you think about it.

But you've been playing along with it all, keeping your mouth shut and saying *please* and *thank you* at every turn. If there's one thing Star taught you it was how to sell people dreams. Star had all kinds of muthafuckas walking in his door, some looking to do things for him, others looking for him to do things for them. The key was to make it seem like you needed them as much as they needed you. Use words like *family* and *crew* and *patna* and they'll do anything for you. You knew what it took to wear the crown. But you wouldn't have cared enough to do what it took to keep it.

When it came down to it, the shadows were a world where you didn't want to live. You had been a guest there way too long, and God had given you a free shot at going completely free. So you moved from there to here, from the capital of the North to the capital of the South on an eighteen-hour train trip that let you sleep better than you have since.

As the goal is to keep up appearances, you got yourself the lamest hooptie you could find, an economy-size '88 Honda CRX. You paid for four years of off-campus tuition in traveler's checks and made your down payment with a money or-der that turned heads when you bought it at that check cashing spot out in College Park. The rest is in a box at the bank down the street. You'll need a job soon to make your income look clean. Something quiet. Something that "normal" people would do. You're "normal" now, after all. You have to remember that.

Ms. Angel fills her throat with one dick and takes another deep into her pussy. You are both mesmerized. Maybe you will see her at the club or some grocery store, or even better, doing a feature dance run at Magic City or one of the other high-end strip joints in town. Sure, you can't afford her, and sure, there's something a little lame about going after what could literally be hundreds of men. But just there, in the grip of the fantasy, when you've got no girl and no friends and when you're in a town you know about as well as the back of a stranger's hand two towns over, she's a nice little diversion from the day-to-day bullshit. But dreams can only take you so far.

You stand up from the couch since your gracious host seems to be bracing himself for the cum shots due to arrive in a matter of moments. The door is calling you. You need to breathe.

Everyone around here still calls it Ashby Street, though the city has officially renamed it Joseph Lawry. They did the same thing with Stewart Avenue a bunch of years back, naming it International Parkway to try to make the world forget that the hoes used to work it and that Club Nikki's used to be right there. A lot of phat asses in this town. Too bad you can't have 'em all.

The drive-thru to Ms. Winner's, the chicken joint, is packed like sardines. They give you a gallon of sweet tea with ten pieces of chicken. Nothin' better than that shit when you've got the munchies and don't want to go too far.

There isn't a cloud in the sky as you walk up the hill, passing the college gym on the left. If Brooklyn College had a sports team you didn't know about it. Here they've got football and basketball and tennis courts and more black broads than all of Brooklyn combined. They took almost all of your credits too, which means that you can still graduate in four. Like the old saying goes: The Lord moves in mysterious ways.

Your cousin explained that there used to be a bunch of projects next to the I-20 underpass but that the school bought them and made them into affordable housing. The only sounds you can hear are passing cars and the little yells of small girls playing double dutch in a parking lot, their skinny legs moving at the speed of light. Soon they won't have time for these kinds of games as they'll learn to go after whichever man can buy them the most.

You and Chief had made a science out of dropping water balloons on double dutch girls from the open window on the fourth-floor stairwell back in the gardens. You liked to make them scream and curse even though they never saw who did it. It's crazy—just a few years after that, you were both fucking those same chicks and trying to cover them in something other than water.

You come up a steep hill past the broke-down supermarket and the community center with the park on the other side. You see drugstores and banks. A homeless man dances on a corner, hoping to score change in his Dunkin' Donuts cup. He almost seems happy to be there. Everybody seems happy to be here, like they just made it through a plane crash the night before or something.

If you were to head straight you'd find yourself in the no-man's-land called East Point, a place where you've heard it's good to have friends, where you shouldn't roll on the solo. So you don't. When in Rome you do whatever it takes to keep you and yours from getting your ass kicked.

You turn left onto Cascade. There's a man in a full suit and hat in ninety-degree weather speaking into a microphone about how the Lord is the only one who can save us from damnation. You wonder why those people think that yelling on the street is going to convince anybody. The only people you follow are those who live by example.

A half a block later you're entering what they call the West End Mall, a series of half-assed stores and shops that wouldn't pose a threat to any mall in Brooklyn. There's a wig shop and an athletic store, a 99-cent spot and a record shop. Plus there's a pizza place and a couple of stalls that have shit like incense and hair grease.

You wonder how in the hell this place has been standing for so long. You wonder what it's like to grow up in a country-ass city like this one. But you have to admit it's been good to see this many smiles, this many people asking how you are on general principle. It melts that cold feeling that's been with you ever since that last night in Brooklyn. It helps you to feel normal, even though you know in your heart that you'll never be normal again.

You're sitting on the kind of cake that could have you living it up at some club with some round chocolate booty grinding you. You could be driving up 85, the summer giving you a whole new layer of caramel. Instead, you park yourself on a bench and just watch the people go by.

There are shapely sets of legs and potbellies, perfect asses pushing out from stretch pants and poom-poom shorts, baby carriages with squeaky wheels and cooing kids. A mall security guard the size of two Biggies makes his rounds, securing shit that in your mind no one would ever try to steal. This is your new life, kid. You better get used to it.

"Somebody sittin' here?" she asks.

You look up to see a pair of eyes of the lightest brown, with a weave to match. B-cup titties are pushed together to make them look like a C. You can't see the ass but the hips are perfect, the toes French-manicured and painted a glittery gold. She's definitely from in-town. But that's not altogether a bad thing.

"Nah," you say.

She plops down, holding a small bag from the greeting card shop in the mall.

"So why you sittin' heah lookin' all sad?" she asks. Her voice is honey-coated with that real strong Atlanta twang. The vowels are extra long, the consonants extra short.

"I'm just takin' a minute," you say. "Lookin' at the people."

"Ain't no people worth lookin' at heah." She grins.

"Then why you sittin' down next to me?"

"You ain't from heah, is you?"

You shake your head.

"New York supposed to have a tidal wave or sumthin'?"

"What you mean?" you ask, surprised that she picked up on your accent so quickly.

"Seem like it's more a you down heah than us."

"A decent house might cost you close to a million in Brooklyn."

"Do it come with a pool?"

You laugh, not knowing whether or not she's serious. But from the looks of her, you're pretty sure she's never been above the Mason-Dixon. She may have never even been out of this neighborhood. But she still seems pretty smart, all things considered.

"Nah," you answer. "But these days you can

usually sell it for more than you paid. Problem is, most people ain't got a million dollars."

"I know that's right," she says.

You glance down at her purse and see that she smokes Parliaments. Anything above Newports says you've got class. As she adjusts the heel on one of her shoes, you can see they're from Nine West. Nothing to write home about. But at least her wedges didn't come off some discount rack.

"What's your name?" you ask her.

"Jennifer."

"Jenifa oh Jenny," you say, remembering that De La Soul song Will used to play all the time.

"What?"

"It's a song my boy used to play."

"Oh, you mean the De La Soul one?"

You nod.

"My sista played that shit to death back in the day. I think she used to sing it to me when I was little."

"How old are you?" Anything above seventeen keeps you away from a case.

"Twun-ee," she says. "So what you 'bout to do?"

"Head back to my cousin's."

"And where he stay at?"

Something inside of you flips on the caution switch.

"Not far. What about you?"

She thinks on it for a moment. "Not far," she grins.

"Then we should get up sometime."

"We should."

She writes her number on the back of a store receipt. Her cursive is pretty. Or prettier than yours at least.

"What time you gonna be home?" you ask.

"If you call I'll answer, no matter where I'm at."

You tell her your name and you shake hands like it was some kind of a business meeting. She gets up before you, probably just to show you the ass you've been trying to peek at. It's like a globe, the kind of thing that would give Will a heart attack, even if he can't fuck her anymore.

For a moment you daydream about a strip of thong resting between her ass cheeks, about what it would be like to grip them while she's on top of you. You want to know how she sounds when she comes. You want to feel those glittery nails grinding into your back.

Then you think of Her and try to push those thoughts away. The same shit can't happen twice— but that doesn't mean you're not paranoid that it still might.

2.

"And we made it, muthafucka!" Duronté screams, a little too excited for winning a single hand of Spades when he's still down 200 in a 500 game.

Meechie is a 5'10" dude with a crazy Afro and a slight limp from when he got hit by a car when he was eight. He's the color of peanut butter and doesn't talk much.

Alonzo is putting himself through grad school by working in the street. So when he's not making runs for Duronté, he's writing papers and hitting the books. You get along with him best for obvious reasons.

Jamar is only seventeen, about to start his last year of high school. He's the driver. He never carries any product, or a pistol, or anything else. He's strictly transportation. He's also your partner in the game, and a damn good one at that.

"Don't tell me you needed your New York cousin to come down South and spank yo' ass," you joke.

There are bottles of Icehouse on the table and a

nice-sized blunt is going around. The Falcons are playing Detroit in the preseason but no one is paying the game any mind.

"Fuck you 'dun sun' ass, nigga!" your cousin yells back, his words starting to slur.

"Hey, hey, y'all family," Alonzo interrupts, trying to sound like Tré from *Boyz N the Hood*.

Everybody laughs. Then Duronté's phone rings.

You can tell it's business because playtime goes out the window. Either he's got a buyer on the line or it's Keyshia Cole saying that she ain't got no panties on. Either way he's pacing.

"I don't know if I can get it that fast," he says into the receiver. The fingers on his other hand fidget. "I'll call you back in a hour, all right? Out."

"Fuck is up?" Alonzo asks.

"You know Reggie over in Candlewood?"

Everyone in the room nods but you.

"Nigga says he's on short, something about his boy gettin' pulled over for a DUI with a good five pounds in the trunk."

This story is the kind of stupidity that makes your skin crawl. But this ain't your operation. So you only speak when spoken to as far as the business is concerned.

"Fuck that got to do with you?" Jamar asks.

"He wants to buy five off me."

"Shit, do you have five?" Alonzo asks.

"It's *all* we got," Meechie says.

That spider sense of yours gets your head a tingling. The way you look at it, this is all a little too convenient.

"Says he'll give me double the wholesale price. I could do it and re-up with Dale tomorrow."

"Hell fuckin' yeah!" Jamar all but yells. "That's what I'm talkin' about."

This is where you have to intervene.

"Where you know this nigga from?" you ask, sliding your chair back from the table to show that you're serious.

"Since high school. We caught up this bitch that was tryin' to play us both. Then we ended up sellin' around the same time. Not much of shit. Dimes and dubs mostly, whatever we could get off the major niggas."

"He ever called you for help before?" you continue.

"Nah, but I don't think he ever needed to."

"He got a dude carrying that much weed in one car? That's somebody he has to trust. And the dude he trusts gets fucking drunk on a run?"

"You think this shit is a setup?" Alonzo asks, as if those kinds of things don't ever happen in the illegal drug business.

"I don't know what it is," you say. "But the shit don't feel right to me."

"But if you wrong, we pass up on some real paper," Jamar says.

"You ain't passin' up on shit, lil' man."

Jamar turns to your cousin, looking for permission to break bad. Duronté's expression lets him know that your words matter.

"What if Jamar's right though?" Alonzo asks.

You could be taking yourself way too seriously in this regard. In truth, you don't know shit about these people. You don't really know shit about the weed business other than what you've overheard in a whole other city. But you ain't no monster either, and there ain't no way in hell you can let some blood of yours walk into a trap unprepared.

"I just don't think you should go out there on the solo to do this. You take some people with you, more than one car and a little something just in case these cats wanna get the party live."

The rest of the room thinks this over.

"And I say we leave Jamar here."

"Why the fuck you wanna do that?" Jamar pouts.

"Because if anything happens, if we get busted, if it turns into a shootout, we got a man and a car back here to come in for the rescue or at least bail us out."

They all look at each other like you're some kind of a genius. It feels good to be control. It feels good to have that little bit of influence, that little bit of power.

"And we're gonna need more than one pistol," you add.

Meechie cracks a weird kind of smile. "That ain't gonna be a problem."

"But before we go to war and all," your cousin says, "let's make sure we got what they need."

And that's how it starts. Duronté and crew start making calls to their various stashes to tell them to put a hold on the inventory. Then Alonzo goes out to make the grab. Meechie heads off to get the heat. And the three of you watch videos on BET.

Duronté sets the meet at some fleabag motel out by the airport. He rents the room, which gives him an advantage of having the whole area checked out before Reggie gets there. Nine times out of ten this whole thing is going to be simple. That feeling you have is probably the same feeling you get about just about everything these days.

But there's another voice in your head, one that says you shouldn't even be giving advice, that you should get yourself a hotel room for the week—until your end is ready. Shit, you've got the money. You should get in your little Honda and wheel it away. This isn't your problem. You're normal now. You're about to start school. You need to put your past far behind you in favor of a nice and safe future.

But at the same time, you were always pretty bad at telling people no.

By midnight you're sitting shotgun in Duronté's ride, a '78 Malibu with a candied copper paint job sitting on Ds. Alonzo's following you and Meechie's going to meet you at the car wash.

"Personally, I don't think this shit is about nuthin' but makin' money," Duronté says as he fires up a Black and Mild. "I mean, it ain't like we talkin' bout heroin."

"Yeah, but you is talking about money, and we all know what niggas will do for money."

"I know that's the truth. But if he wanted to go at us he coulda just hit us at the crib."

"Yeah, but what if he ain't lie about losing his stash? What if he just ain't got the money to pay for it so he's gonna jack you to get what he need?"

"But it's just weed. Gettin' weed is like gettin' milk at the sto' around heah."

You give him nothing but a nod as your two-car caravan makes its way onto the interstate. After that it's nothing but headlights and medians for close to a half-hour. Duronté switches the song in his changer every other minute. Just as you're getting used to the track he jumps into something else, from Outkast to T.I. to Archie Bell and James Brown. He's nervous. You both are.

Your cousin bought into a car wash as a result of getting four numbers out of five in the state lottery, which earned him $100,000 the summer he turned nineteen. After taxes he had about sixty Gs left, which his mother convinced him to invest in something (after he gave her a nice piece, of course). With that he bought his ride, two bricks of hydro, and into this place, which some old school rapper had run into the ground by overcharging and undermaintaining. Duronté was sitting on the exact amount the guy needed to give the place a full overhaul and start back at zero.

He gets fifteen percent of the monthly take after taxes and permission to have his people sell tree to whoever's looking for it. He might be a little over the top sometimes, but your cousin is definitely not stupid.

There isn't a light on anywhere as you and Alonzo park in the rear. Duronté types a code into a lit keypad and two security floodlights come on, revealing what looks like any other car wash in the middle of nowhere. He puts a key in the lock and heads inside.

The three of you move down a flight of stairs and into what looks like a small office. There's a TV and a pool table and an old-ass arcade game called Centipede. You remember it from when you were little but you never actually played yourself. This is the staff rec room. Employees come down here on their lunch breaks and to change at the beginning of shifts. The pool table was Duronté's idea. The whole setup is so nice that it makes you wonder why in the hell he's selling weed.

It's another half-hour before Meechie finally gets there carrying a backpack with four different pistols and, of all things, a grenade.

"The fuck you bring this for?" Alonzo asks Meechie.

"Playboy said it was a bonus. Says he got a whole box of 'em."

"I don't think we're gonna need no shit like that."

You have your Glock handy and Duronté has his .45, so it's really Alonzo and Meechie's show. Alonzo picks a Beretta 9. Meechie grabs both of the .380s. Duronté tucks the bag with the rest in a lockable file cabinet. It's 1:15 by the time everyone is locked and loaded. It'll take at least thirty to get to the motel. So the fifteen will be all you have to give the place a good look, which should be enough.

"I gotta ask you a question," you say, breaking the silence on the ride from I-20 to 285.

"Wassup?" Duronté replies.

"Why you in this weed thing if you making cake from the car wash? Is it really worth it for you?"

"You gotta have a lotta different hustles, playa. I mean, yeah, that car wash shit bring in a couple grand a month. But see, I put that shit away. What if I have a kid or I need to get outta town or whatever? That check does right to my lil' money market account. I make investments and shit. But this right heah, this shit is about who I am, about bein' somebody. I'm the man to come to off Ashby Street. When school start up, all them college boys and girls be at my do' for their dub and they ounces. They got me at they parties, sometimes even up in they dorm rooms. You know, one time this dude from Cali had me at his graduation dinner? I mean, that's the real shit. That's juice. That's livin' and bein' young. If I had a way to do more, if I could get my hands on somethin' even bigger and be fresh to death for real . . . I'd do that too."

Duronté is both smarter and dumber than you thought. On one hand he's looking toward the future, thinking about what matters beyond the here and now. On the other he's caught up in getting props, in being known, and that's a losing proposition. In the end, being known only makes you a target.

Your three cars pull into an almost empty lot just out past the ugly Bankhead Court Apartments. They seem familiar, as if you might have seen them in a video once or something. But the motel in question looks even worse than those projects, like some shit Norman Bates would hit the gas to get past.

The night manager is missing two fingers on his right hand. From what you can tell, it looks like a war wound. Some mortar blast or a mine or shrapnel. He is gray all over, even the hair on his arms, and he looks like his mind is somewhere else as he takes your forty dollars and hands your cousin a metal key with the number 13 attached.

The whole place is ranch-style, which means it's all on one floor. Duronté gives the boys the number and you drive around and park in the designated space that comes with the room.

Taking your advice, Duronté tells Meechie to park by the room two units over from yours and to wait there on stealth. Alonzo parks behind the trash dumpsters at the far end of the parking lot with his engine running. If it's some kind of a setup, there's help in two different places. Then, you'll have Duronté's back on the inside.

In the middle of all of this, you find yourself thinking about family. In a way, Duronté and Mabel are all that you have. You don't want to trust them because everyone you've trusted has ended up dead. You don't even want to believe that you're related, because you don't want to pull them into what it took you almost everything to get out of. But listening to your cousin and thinking about who your real parents were, you know that you are the spawn of hustlers. Your people have never played it straight. You have always taken the angles. You have always tried to buck the system.

You think about your old man, or what little

you can remember of him and your mama. There was always some stranger coming by the house, always some banging on the door at a late hour. You don't remember guns but you remember the smell of weed and incense mixed together. That smell has followed you everywhere since.

The room is an absolute bug farm. An army of ants climbs one wall to go through a tiny crack in the ceiling. The sheets look like they haven't been changed in weeks. The sign out front should say, *Truckers, Johns, and Dealers Welcome.* Which one of those are you? Or are you all of the above?

2 a.m. comes and goes like nothing. Then it's 2:30 and then 3. Duronté calls Reggie and there's no answer. But just as he closes his phone, the room phone rings and he rushes to answer.

It doesn't take much for you to tell that who-ever the caller is has just scared the fuck out of your cousin. He holds the phone to his ear for less than thirty seconds before dropping it back into the cradle.

"What the fuck is up?" you ask.

"He says what you're looking for is in the trash dumpster out in the lot."

You know what's inside before you even close the front door behind you and Duronté. It becomes even clearer as you start across the lot. Meechie drives from around back and Alonzo turns his engine off. You're glad Jamar is back at the house. He doesn't need to see this, unless he has to.

You can smell the blood as you flip the thick plastic off the steel container. There are four men inside. And though you don't know them, the rest of your people do.

"Oh shit. That's fuckin' Reggie!" Alonzo yells, perhaps too loudly considering the fact that someone might be able to pin accessory beefs on all of you.

The bodies are piled from the largest, a fat boy who barely looks twenty, to Reggie's, a 5'6" kid with too many tattoos, sort of a light-skinned Lil' Wayne without the dreads.

"Who did this shit?" Meechie asks. None of you have turned away from the bodies, even though most people would be hurling or running.

Their throats have been slit, as if four men with knives just walked up behind them and did them away with single slashes. Reggie has a note pinned to his chest. You snatch if off of him as if you're worried that he's going to wake up.

"What it say?" Duronté asks.

The letters are written big and clear: *Your House.*

Maybe it wasn't such a good idea to leave Jamar there alone.

Duronté's in fifth gear on the way out of the parking lot and the others are right behind you. More bodies. It's ridiculous that you didn't even flinch, that they didn't flinch. Maybe it's because none of you want to believe that something this fucked up could actually go down. I mean, hell, at least a shootout would have been something you'd have more control over. Four people are dead and some poor high school kid could be next.

Duronté's speedometer is pushing past eighty when you tell him to slow down. Cobb County is no fucking place to get pulled over, especially since you forgot to put your guns in the trunk. That's three years in jail for speeding. You tell him to calm down, that at least it wasn't any of his own people.

"But it's still a nigga I know," he says.

You can see how he has a point, but he's not looking at the bigger picture. Whoever did this knew where you were, which means that Reggie told them. But the bigger question is why. If it was a straight robbery, why kill everyone? Plus, knives are sloppy. Knives come out of anger. Someone was trying to set an example in a place where Duronté could see it plain as day. The question was . . . why?

There's a 850 CSi with Illinois plates parked right in front Duronté's place. You tell your cousin to cruise past and further down the street. Alonzo and Meechie seem to know to follow suit. You park as quietly as possible and form a circle out in the street to put together a new plan.

It's the same as at the motel. Duronté gives Meechie the key to the back door and tells him to cover it. If he hears shots, he comes in ready to blast. Alonzo stays out front with his engine running. You and your cousin go in the front.

You figure that if shots had already gone off, someone would have called the cops, even in this neighborhood. If Jamar's sliced up . . . well, that's another story. Your gun feels so heavy now, like that ring around Frodo's neck. You don't want to pull it out. You don't want to pull any more triggers.

You take the keys from Duronté to open the front door, but it's already cracked. You push it open to see Jamar tied to a chair with telephone cords. The crotch of his pants is stained with piss. He looks like he's the dead walking the earth.

On either side of him are two men in suits. Both are tall and slender, but one is dark-skinned and the other more of a toasted-almond color. They're both in their thirties, maybe older.

"You Duronté?" one of the men asks.

"I am," your cousin proclaims, tapping his chest with a fist like a Southern gangsta Tarzan. You would clown him for it if not for the circumstances.

"I guess you got our message," Almond says.

"And why was the message for him?" you interrupt. You want to see what these suits are made of.

"Because he stands to win where Reggie lost."

"Look, that shit wasn't over my weed, was it?"

Darker laughs.

"Not hardly. He owed us some money for some other product that he tried to get away with not paying. We couldn't let that go unpunished."

"But why'd you hit him at our thing? Why not before?"

"Because we need a replacement," Almond says.

"A replacement for what?"

"Reggie was moving a nice amount of weight for us. Good quality. Good price. He was moving away from the weed business. Not enough money in it for all the headaches."

"And before we continue," Darker says, "we didn't touch your boy here. He did the pissing the minute we came through the door."

You want to laugh again but you force a straight face.

"We can give you a list of every piece of real estate Reggie had, and the workers who are still loyal to us," Almond explains. "All we need is someone to oversee the operation."

You immediately think about the conversation the two of you just had in the car, about opportunity presenting itself. Now here it is. You know he's churning it through his brain like butter.

"What's the split?" your cousin asks, actually licking his lips after the words hit the air. They have him without having him. But they don't have you.

"No split," Darker says. "You buy at our price and sell for what you want."

You can almost picture the erection in the boy's drawers. He's no longer thinking that his partner from high school and his crew are now dead. He doesn't ask *anything* about his crew.

"I'm in," he says. He will think on this moment for the rest of his life.

Darker produces a business card that Duronté reads.

"That's the number you use for everything," Almond says. "That's the gateway to *Lifestyles of the Rich and Famous*."

You get the impression that this is their job. They are the spokespeople for a someone else far too important to stop by broke-down cribs on Ashby Street, a someone else who unfortunate people never see—until it's too late.

3.

It still surprises you that people can be so blind and so stupid. But this time you know enough to understand that you can only save yourself. So as you watch Duronté shake hands on a deal that you know will spell disaster, you figure that the best thing for you to do is get out of the lane before this whole thing puts its nuts on your forehead.

At the same time, walking out during this negotiation is a one-way ticket to a casket. The Illinois twins might take it as a sign of disrespect and slit your throat before you can turn the key in your car. More importantly, one of your only living relatives could hate your forever. Out of the two, that's the harder pill to swallow.

So you stand there while the three of them finish things up, looking like the loyal soldier. Neither member of the twins looks in your direction at all, only at the freshly caught fly in a web you know is made of nothing but deceit.

"Do you have an e-mail address?" Almond asks.

Duronté grins. "What you think, that I'm in

the Dark Ages and shit? Hell yeah, I got e-mail."

"Then we'll send you all the info you need."

Drop points and corners by e-mail? You're wondering who these guys work for and why somebody this high-powered can't find himself people more experienced in the dope game.

You also know that there's no way that Reggie's crew is going to jump onboard without things getting shaken up. Even Keyser Söze doesn't have that much juice. But Duronté's eyes are completely glazed over with ambition. He's like that dude in the Shakespeare play you read once, the guy who killed the king just because the witches told him to. But the witches didn't tell him everything.

Your cousin shakes hands with these dudes like they just sold him life insurance. You watch them walk out the front, get into the Beemer, and drive off like business as usual. Duronté cracks a smile.

"That went better than I thought."

You have the impulse to backslap him. But you remind yourself that this isn't your problem, that you're just a houseguest, that your crib will be ready in a matter of days and then you can go live there. Shit, you could get a room at Pascal's down the way and ride it out.

"You think so, right?" he asks you, noticing the uncomfortable silence.

"This is your show," you explain. "You gotta make the decisions."

"But you my cousin, man. And you know the game. I can't make no moves without you."

This is when Alonzo comes up the walk and Meechie enters through the rear.

"I seen 'em drive off," Alonzo says, a little out of breath from jogging up the street. "What the fuck happened?"

"They made me a offer I couldn't refuse."

He tells the whole story like it's straight out of a comic book. He adds more tension and suspense, making it seem as if he ran two punks out of his crib after he made them give him a piece of their thing. And of course the boys eat it up, as homeboys do, because to think or say otherwise is the worst kind of hood sacrilege a man can commit.

They'll have the entire city on lock. They'll get muscle, more guns, as they know plenty of others who'll want to be down. Blunts are rolled. Brews are cracked. That damn Ayana Angel porno comes on again. This is their night. But it most definitely is not yours.

You excuse yourself after an hour or so. You say you've got a broad to go see and step out on the porch to make a call. But for a while you just sit there, watching the occasional lightning bug float through the sky and listening to the sound of a single cricket off in the distance. Eventually you flip the phone open and dial your only current shot at pussy in the greater Atlanta area.

She is wide awake when you hear her voice, even though it's pushing 4 in the morning. The TV is on in the background. When you ask, she says that it's *Cheaters*. She loves watching people get busted, especially black people. Because even when the brothers get caught red-handed they still deny it for the sake of the cameras, thinking that their reputations, that their sense of game, are far more important than the love they feel for the women they betrayed.

You ask her why she's still awake and she says that she always is, that she's been a night person ever since she was little, that she only moves around in the day because it's the time where people have to get things done. You ask what she does for a living and she says, "A little bit of everything." It really wouldn't surprise you if that actually meant that she sold dubs herself.

When she asks why you're up, you say that you and your boys closed down Pleasers on a Sunday night. It was the only place where you could drink and where the dancers were decent for a five-dollar table dance. She asks if you saw any girls you liked. You say you got a dance from a tall girl the color of tar with a booty that felt perfect when she gave you a dance.

She says that lap dancing is against the law.

You say, "So is smokin' weed, but when has that stopped anybody?"

She laughs. You laugh back. She asks where you are and you tell her. She says she's close and wants to know if you'll go for a drive. You say yes. She gives you the address.

You think she's gonna have jokes about your little economy car. But as you pull up to the address she gave you, you really don't care anymore. She's wearing a little half-top with spaghetti straps and jeans that look painted on. The pants match the blue in her jelly flip-flops. Her weave is tied up in a big ponytail. You notice a blond streak on one side that you don't think you saw before.

"You smoke?" she asks after she clicks her seat belt tight. You nod. She has a sack of weed with a brownish color in one hand and a little thing of papers in the other. The smile she gives you is devilish. "I thought so," she says.

You drive up to Cascade and then out past the park off of Peeples Street. You pass the Long John Silver's and the Kroger and all the crackheads on Richland Road. That soul food place, The Beautiful, is all dark, as it should be so early in the morning.

"What's your middle name?" she asks you.

"Where did that come from? You don't even know my last name."

"Your last name's easier to find out," she says.

She's wearing this perfume that you should remember, this scent that you've smelled on someone else somewhere else. It still smells so good.

"I ain't gonna make my middle name that easy then," you say.

"A'ight then," she chuckles. Rick James is on the radio. "Fire and Desire."

She turns it up. She knows all the words even though the song is older than she is. Shit, it's even older than you are. For some reason, this is the moment when you remember that you'll be going to school with kids younger than you, that none of them will truly know who you are or what you've been doing. You will envy them because 99.9 percent of them don't have blood on their hands, none of them have an eternity in the fiery depths to look forward to.

You pull onto a side street and she rolls and lights. You pass the joint back and forth. The high kicks in quickly. The tension relaxes. The truth is that you just want to lay your head in her lap, that you want someone to make you forget about four more bodies in a dumpster. But there's no way she could possibly understand any of that. There's no way she can understand who you really are.

"So how come you ain't got a man?"

"'Cuz most men ain't shit. And the one's that are don't know how to handle me."

You look her up and down. Her words make you want to put your fingers inside of her. You want to see her swallow you whole while you make her come by playing with her clit. That's what nights like this are for. Right?

"I think I can take it," you say.

"We'll see."

You lean in to kiss her and she gives you her lips. They are as soft as a baby's flesh. You pull her to you with one hand while the other brushes her breast. You can feel a thick nipple harden against your thumb. Each touch makes you crave more. She brings a hand to your crotch and begins to rub slowly. You reach under the bra and lift it over the breast it protects. Then you bring your lips down to it. She moans.

You try to work on her jeans but she stops you. Instead, she goes to work on your own, unbuttoning and unzipping, reaching into the slit of your boxers to pull out what is now long past hard. She lowers her face without your asking. Her breath is hot as those lovely lips seal the deal. Through the windshield the sun is beginning to shine. It is truly a brand new day.

"What the fuck you talkin' bout?!"

You can't say that you didn't expect him to act like this. You just didn't think he'd wild out in a Waffle House on a Monday afternoon. There is half a pecan waffle in front of you and some hash browns. You can still smell Jenny's perfume on you.

"I can't do it," you say.

He wants you to help him become the new kingpin of Atlanta (as if there were a single reigning champ), even if there can be no such thing anymore.

"I cain't do this by myself."

"You said yeah by yourself," you reply.

"That's just 'cuz I thought you was with me all the way."

"Look, I told you I'm down here to go to school. I'm done wit' all that shit."

"Then why wuz you even with us last night? Why the fuck you givin' me advice?"

"'Cuz you family and I didn't wanna see you or your boys get hurt. Because I knew you hadn't never been in no shit like this before."

"And now you gon' back the fuck out when we can finally make some real cake."

"Cake ain't everything, D. It ain't. You let them muthafuckas sell you the fuckin' dream without askin' no questions. Reggie's boys ain't gon' just follow you *because*. And even if they do, what about the cops, the DEA? You ain't got no payroll money like that. You ain't got no inside info. You do this and you just another nigga on a corner, plain and simple."

"But how can I not do it now? You seen what they did to Reggie. How am I gonna back out?"

You don't really have a particular answer for this one. If it was some stranger on the street, you'd probably tell him he was shit out of luck. But this is your cousin, your *only* cousin. You've never turned your back on family, even when they turned their backs on you. So how can you now?

"I don't know how much difference I can make anyway."

"I just need you there, man. You know, you been through shit. If them Chicago niggas had tried somethin', you had the plan in effect right there. I mean, I can handle the business part, but I ain't so good with the chess board, you know?"

You hesitate, because you know that once the words hit the air you can't take them back. By saying what you're going to say, you are putting a target on your own head. You are potentially fingerprinting yourself and standing before a judge to be tried as an accessory.

Duronté doesn't know about the money you have left. The truth is, he doesn't even really know who you are. He just sees you as a gateway to being something all the music videos have made to be more glamorous than it is. You know that those glory days are over. The weight still moves but there ain't no monopolies. People get killed. People get third strikes. A lot of funerals both inside and out.

None of this feels right. But with all the shit on your conscience, all the demons swirling around your head because of what happened that last night in Brooklyn, maybe it's time you do something for somebody else, even if it costs.

"Look man. I'll do what I can."

He gives you this look like he wants to hug you. But the rules of men don't allow such things. So you pay the bill and hop into your cousin's ride. You've got a business to build.

4.

"I'm a muthafuckin' soldier," the dude says. Maybe he's twenty. About 5'9", 160. He kind of looks like T.I. except he has cornrows. He's wearing an oversized Falcons jersey and a 4XL white T on a body that should be wearing a large. He's the tenth person that's come to see you in the last few hours.

You pretend to be playing pool while he and Duronté discuss the whole membership thing. All of the core crew are there (even Jamar got a promotion as a result of the new development in your cousin's business). So now you need lieutenants to manage the various venues.

Luckily for Duronté, Reggie didn't do a lot of corners. He mostly worked out of stores, dry cleaners, and other businesses. It was an even bigger surprise that all of his people went along with the switch-over without much of a shake-up. Maybe it had to do with the fact that Duronté had a rep for doing good business with weed, an area that Alonzo is now completely in charge of. Duronté's put you in for twenty percent of whatever he gets, which means that your legit job is out the window for the time being.

There are still five days until registration at school. Your crib will be ready in about twenty-four hours, which means you have a week to put furniture in it while you help your cousin set up shop. Things have been so hectic that you haven't even had a chance to return Jennifer's calls. You text her though, and she seems to understand. After all, it's barely been a day.

School was so close just a day ago, but now it's kind of off in the distance, like summer vacation in April. Now the whole thing is keeping your cousin from getting killed, even if you're not so sure you can.

B.I. (the fake-ass T.I.) pulls Duronté into a hug and makes his exit back up the stairwell, never giving you a second look.

You're glad about that, as the last thing you want is to be a known face in what is soon to become an organization.

"What you think of him?" Duronté asks.

"I think he's fulla shit," you say, as you put the eight ball in the corner pocket, even though the stick is seriously warped. "But he'll do."

"I figured I'll put him in the car with Jamar, have him show him the ropes."

You can do nothing but shake your head. But then, after a minute, you explode: "Nigga, are you out of your goddamn mind? You know this muthafucka for like ten seconds and you put him in a car with one of your main people, the one who pissed himself when the Chicago twins showed up?"

There's another long pause.

"I guess I didn't think about it like that."

Family is meaning less and less to you by the second.

"Let him run for Meechie for a while," you suggest.

Meechie is in charge of the stash at Golden Glide, the skating rink. He needs somebody to keep an eye out. Sure, it's the kind of job you'd use some sixteen-year-old for, but in a time crunch you can up the pay and make it worth his while, until he proves some loyalty. Then he moves up.

"You got it." Duronté nods in approval, as if his approval is the kind of thing that makes you feel better. Part of you already wants to ask for higher percentage. That part knows the longer you stick around, the more of his messes you'll have to clean up after. But you keep that part in check.

Ten seconds later, Jamar comes running down the stairs.

"It's here," he announces, his heart beating out of his chest.

"It" is the product, and here and now, just after 10, Old National is quiet enough. The two of you

s boy up the stairs to the back, where the
ust coming in.

ve got about five guys there to make sure
the shipment comes in okay, dudes who have been
around the block, done a little time on weapons
charges. The oldest, Frank, is in his thirties and
did a long stretch for manslaughter. Most of them
came from Meechie, one from Alonzo. They seem
reliable enough, their eyes darting every which
way in search of potential threats.

The first twenty kilos come in courtesy of a
school milk truck. Two designated crates (blue instead of the usual gray) have the powder packed
into empty milk cartons. There's not a whole lot
to carry, but with everything in the worst kind of
transition, you can't be too careful.

Meechie is out at the rink and Alonzo is back
at Duronté's place on weed detail. The driver, a
fat man whose race is hard to figure out, comes
around back and struggles to slide the trailer open.
You and Jamar step in to get the two crates, which
are both light as feathers.

One goes into Duronté's car and the other into
yours. Jamar rides shotgun with you, Frank with
your cousin. The drive to the chemist out in Stone
Mountain is going to be pretty long.

It's both good and bad that there's so much distance between things. It's good because all the different shops aren't connected, which means that

any problem at one place can't easily spread to any of the others without a drive. It's bad because if something jumps off, you can't get there quickly, especially when there's so few people in management positions. You'll have to work on that, sooner than later.

You don't know anything about making crack, though you've heard it's a lot simpler than heroin. But little Jamar apparently does—some cousin of his had some uncle who did the baking soda thing long ago.

You soon need fiends for the taste test. But that's one kind of staffing that won't be in short supply.

You've been missing New York since the day you left. There aren't enough lights here, not enough sounds. Sometimes you think you're waiting in a vacuum, almost like sitting in bumper-to-bumper traffic on the Jersey Turnpike. You can remember making runs with your foster dad from the Ikea in Elizabeth, and that one time you went with him to visit his great-aunt down by Trenton. In traffic there was nothing to do but listen to the radio (or the commercials, depending on the station) or to your government-appointed old man ramble on and on about how things used to be out here. You miss his little lectures. But you really miss *him*.

You also miss Brooklyn, the Caribbean place

up the street that was better at jerking off than they were at jerk chicken. You miss your truck, which has most likely been auctioned off to some eighteen-year-old by now as part of a seized-property sale. You miss watching the fireworks from across the river on the Fourth of July. You miss the only place you've ever really known, and now it's gone, dead to you all, because of one blowjob too many. The suck that emptied a thousand clips, or whatever you want to call it.

From what you've heard, Stone Mountain, Georgia was once a haven for the upwardly mobile. Nothing but green lawns, nice-sized houses, and neighbors who invited you to barbecues and cocktail parties. But according to Jamar, things have been changing with the new folks moving into the city from all kinds of places.

You've grown up your whole life being taught that New York is the center of the world, that no one can touch you, that the streets you walked on were made of some kind of concrete you couldn't find anywhere else. But in this new place, the world now seems so much bigger, so much more complicated. And it scares you sometimes. It really scares you.

"How much shit you got?" our much-older-than-expected chemist asks. He is 5'3" at best, a small wiry Jewish man with thick glasses and a clubfoot, not exactly the type of "cook" you've been expecting. You imagined some tatted-up dude with his shirt off and a mask over his face.

But the garage seems to be equipped with all that you might need, though ventilation is a question. He points to the electrical vacuuming system built into one of the walls, like the kind of thing they have in chemistry class. It takes toxins out before they come close to killing anyone.

He says he'll need overnight to get it street ready. It's going to cost your cousin five grand, which is quite a hit. The twins didn't tell him that the operation was going to run you some start-up dough. Even with what Duronté has put away, turning a profit is going to cost him. If this was a legit business, he might have to mortgage that car wash to the hilt. But then again, you've only been here for a little bit. You don't know what he has stashed and where.

Duronté pays the man in hundreds and Frank and Jamar take the goods out of the trunks. In twenty-four hours you'll officially be in business, whatever that means.

You're heading down the walk when Duronté's phone rings. He puts it on speaker just in time for us to hear the gunshots and what sounds like Alonzo screaming, then the line goes completely dead.

All four of you stand there for a second, asking yourselves whether or not this might be a joke of some kind. Sure, you're pretty far away from both Halloween and April Fools', but Alonzo could have this much bad taste. That moment doesn't last though.

"Where the fuck is he?" you ask your cousin, who's as frozen as George W. Bush on 9/11.

"My house," he says. Once again, you're going to have to take charge of the situation.

You move as fast as you can back toward the SWATS, a forty-minute run at a speed that threatens to put cops on your tail. With every other breath you're kicking yourself for not trusting your own intuition, for telling family to go fuck themselves and getting involved in yet another losing venture. But here you are, racing to rescue a man you don't even know, even when it could be the worst kind of trap.

You go from the long strip of 85 to 20 to Ashby to Fair and are about to make the turn to Duronté's crib when you see the fire engines and emergency vehicles everywhere. The sky above your cousin's block is gray. There's a house on fire. And it looks like the one you've been staying in.

You can imagine what's going through your cousin's mind in the other car. But since you're in front of him, you set the pace by proceeding at a slow speed, heading up the block and then making a quick turn in the other direction, moving back toward your own house down on Palmetto.

All of a sudden you're thinking of your shoes and your clothes, the only pictures you had of both sets of parents. You're thinking about Alonzo. You hope that he went quickly, a single shot to the head followed by that final scream you all heard. You almost lose control of the wheel when you consider the fact that the cops will be looking for your cousin, that he'll have a dead body to answer questions about, not to mention the several pounds of weed and multiple firearms that will be found on the premises. He's fucked, completely fucked. And you're not far behind.

Your house is dark and quiet, as it should be. Luckily the power's been turned on, but there's no furniture. Still, it's a place where no one would think to find you, a safe house for the time being. You park at the bottom of the hill and walk back up to the place. The others follow suit. Your future is as clear as day: One way or another, blood has to be spilled.

5.

"**M**an, what the fuck?" Duronté yells, as he kicks one of the empty buckets the contractors left behind. It slams against the exposed brick wall and rolls into a corner off in the shadows. Bringing them here was a bad move.

Since there is no furniture, everyone plants his ass on the redone floors. The dishwasher has been fixed and the paint on the ceilings no longer peels. The section of the roof that needed to be reshingled has been taken care of. And there are new windows, to prevent heat loss in the winter.

Now your close-to-ten-thousand-in-repairs is playing host to a gang of killers and dealers grieving over the unexplained loss of a homeboy, the burning down of the crib his body is inside of, and the potential death of a new operation at the hands of men you don't even have voices to identify with.

"Whoever it is, they tryin' to take us out piece by piece," Meechie says, stroking the barrel of the shotgun in his lap. "Maybe that shit with the house was just a warning."

"Warning?" your cousin shouts. "Burnin' down a nigga's house is not a fuckin' warning! We gotta find these muthafuckas! These niggas got to *go!*"

He is bouncing around the living room like some kid on Ritalin. It's like the rest of you aren't even there, as if you perished in the fire along with the rest of his life. And the house itself is just the tip of the iceberg. Mabel is most likely en route to the scene of the crime, where she will have to answer questions about that pungent marijuana scent coming from the fire. And then there's Alonzo's body, to be found with bullets in it, inside of the inferno. She's not going to eat charges like those when she's got to see what happens on *Days of Our Lives* tomorrow afternoon. She'll have to drop Duronté's name.

Then comes the warrant. He's got an alibi for the murder, but telling it straight potentially puts him in the slammer for the bodies at the motel, or a distribution charge if they can get someone to talk.

"You gotta get outta here, D," you say. "If Five-O ain't got you on one thing in this deal, they got you on another, plain and simple. You need to scrape up the cake and get somewhere else until the heat dies down."

"I ain't goin' out like a bitch. Fuck that! We gotta find the muthafuckas that did this shit!"

It's clear to you that your cousin has never

dropped a body, that he doesn't understand how it becomes a death sentence within itself. Snatching a soul from a temple launches a razor-sharp boomerang that will come right back for your own neck. He doesn't understand that getting the trigger men won't do shit but add to the body count, that it will only serve to send more people after you.

"You ain't played this game," you say to him. "Ain't no last level. The shit just keep on goin' until you dead or locked up. Why the fuck you think I'm so pressed to go to school? Why the fuck you think I got the fuck outta Brooklyn?"

"Sound to me like you runnin' outta heart," Frank says.

This is one of those moments where you hate the game even more. As you stand there in front of an old man who just has to fucking test you, you want to remain calm, to stay focused. But then you see those bodies in the dumpster and the fire and your bitch-ass cousin's wide eyes when the Wonder Twins came through his door with the deal of a lifetime. You think back to Star and Will and Her, and the dial to the safe that keeps your anger back starts to spin the opening combination on its own. The lever that opens the door is pushed.

You need a target. You need to establish dominance. Frank will serve a dual purpose.

"The fuck did you say?"

The words stun his ears. He apparently never thought too highly of you. He has apparently been just tolerating you. You've just been the silly nigga that rolls with Duronté.

D is the powerful one and you are the fucking joke.

"You heard me, nigga," he growls. His eyes darken. In a split second he is possessed by the animal that earns him his paycheck.

He starts to stand, but you don't give him the chance. You kick the wind out of his chest and he goes back down, coughing. You could stop there, but then he wouldn't have learned the lesson.

Your kicks turn into stomps. You hold him by the collar of his crew neck, ramming your fist into his face over and over. You kick that Beretta of his across the room. You bring a foot down on his face and hear the crack of his nose bone. Blood comes forth like a faucet, water exploding from what was supposed to be a stone.

You stop when he's just a hair away from passing out. You want him to see you there, standing over him. You want him to understand mercy and loyalty and survival of the fittest.

You can feel the others looking on; any doubts they may have had about your past, about your cousin's devotion to you, end right there. They don't understand that this isn't who you were in

Brooklyn. This is merely what you became on that last night. And now there's no going back.

It takes Frank close to ten minutes to get to his feet. Meechie and Jamar untangle his limbs and grab a wad of paper towels to press against his bleeding nose. He'll need to go to the hospital to have the bone reset. Then he'll either decide to respect you or find someone else to roll with, plain and simple.

Duronté stands behind you speechless as he takes in the whipping you put on the best man he could find to hire. He glances at you with a kind of a fear far beyond the admiration that got the two of you to where you are. This is your moment to do what's needed. This is your moment to take charge of this whole situation.

"You got a ATM card?" you ask Duronté, making sure his eyes meet yours.

He nods.

"Then it's time to get that ticket."

"Ticket for where?"

"Anywhere but here. Cops as much as pull you over for speeding, you're looking at a minimum of five, probably ten." You don't know this for sure, but you want to scare him.

"But ain't shit in my account," he argues. "All that's at the box at the bank, and it ain't open until morning."

For once he has done something smart. But it's

risky. He's gotta take money with him. Even so, waiting until morning means that there will be more cops on alert, maybe even someone at the bank. The minute he walks into that branch, ten plainclothes will take him to the tiles and that's that. Someone else is going to have to handle it.

"9 a.m., right?"

Duronté nods back.

"All right then, where's the key?"

Your cousin looks around the room, scanning the faces of his Cabinet nervously. He's becoming the kind of paranoid he should have been from day one. Now he knows he can't answer my question in the open.

"I got it stashed," he tells you. "We can get it on the way in the morning."

Frank begins to murmur something as he sits there, holding himself. He's looking away from you, out of what seems like embarrassment. At some point you may admit to him that you had to play it dirty, that if you'd let him get to his feet it would have all been over. But not today, as come tomorrow it seems that you'll be running the show yourself, at least for as long as you can handle it.

Everyone else just sits quietly. You're sure that some of the silence is mourning. None of them had been expecting this side of things. None of them had understood just how serious this whole deal was.

"We still gon' try and find him, right?" Jamar asks.

Everybody other than Frank looks to you. Vengeance is their only motivator to stay in this game, as job security just went out the window.

"Hell the fuck yeah, you is!" Duronté answers, even though you're sure the question wasn't addressed to him. "Bring me that muthafucka's head and we can get back to business."

Your cousin's back to being not-so-sharp again. He's back to thinking he's still sitting in the big chair, when you've snatched him out of it to save his life. The bigger question is whether or not you can still save your own.

It's just after 2 when everyone takes off except for you and Duronté. He rolls a joint and the two of you try to hide your fears in the smoke that begins filling the room.

"I didn't think it was gon' be like this," he says, as he lays flat on the floor, spitting a geyser of smoke into the already-hazy air.

"I know you didn't," you say. "I knew you didn't hear me."

"Why didn't you say shit?"

"It's like *The Last Dragon*," you say. "You wanted that glow but you didn't know what came with it. And that shit always comes sooner or later. For you it came sooner."

"But what about Mama?"

"You can't reach out until you got some wiggle room, until you leave the cops an answer to the question."

"What you mean?"

"You find the gun that killed Alonzo, then you find a way to stick the gun to whoever pulled the trigger. You gotta know that whoever did this shit ain't gonna stop. So you know they're gonna go after something else. We gotta beat 'em to the punch, leave 'em someplace where the cops can find them with that gun and connect one thing to the other."

"There ain't gonna be no bullet left after a fire," he argues.

"They find all kindsa shit after a fire," you explain. "Them arson muthafuckas is no joke. But you gotta get rid of the body. Nobody gives a shit about the weed. It's the murder they'll want to clear."

"Where the fuck am I supposed to go in the meantime?"

"I can't help you there."

"I ain't fuckin' wit' Detroit," he says. "But I always wanted to see Memphis. You know, be up there chowin' down on some barbecue and fuckin' wit' the hoes out there. I been wantin' to do that shit ever since I was Hustle and Flow."

You imagine him blowing through town on a Greyhound and getting taken for his dough by some dime-store nigga trying to sell him thirty keys of baking soda. Though maybe you're being too hard on him. Maybe he'll actually survive.

You drift in and out of sleep. The wood floor seems harder than anything you've ever slept on. But it probably has an awful lot to do with your nerves. Since when have you been the one to go hunting down hit squads? Since when have you been stomping out convicted felons just to establish dominance? You're a salmon swimming in shark-infested waters with not a dolphin in sight.

You open your eyes just after 8. Duronté takes a shower but has to put the same drawers and clothes back on, as they're all he has left in the wardrobe department. You have coffee and bacon and eggs at that Waffle House you both like. And then you head to the bank.

You remain calm as a woman who you know is somebody's mama leads you to the basement where the safe deposit boxes are kept. She examines your key as she slips it into the lock next to hers. Then she gives you privacy.

The bills inside aren't organized. They've been stuffed in there in odd increments. Nothing is bound. So you end up stuffing it all into the gym bag you picked up on the way. You slide an empty box back into its container and make your way up out of the branch, walking right past the lady you were supposed to notify when you were taking off. But it's no matter. Neither you nor your cousin will ever set foot in this branch again.

Duronté is sweating bullets when you climb back into the car.

"What the fuck took you so long?"

"You don't know how to fold and stack?"

His face turns red. "Oh," he stutters. "My bad."

"So where it gonna be?"

He gets a one-way ticket to Memphis from Birmingham. The plan is for him to drive to Alabama, sell his car, find a motel for the night, and then cab it to the train station. He buys a prepaid cell from one place and a phone card from another. Then he drops you off at the first MARTA station you come across.

"Handle this for me," he mutters in a way that says he's doing more asking than telling.

"I'ma do what I do," you say with a grin. "Everything's gonna be straight."

He turns onto Piedmont and filters into a stream of busy traffic. You don't watch him leave. You know that if anything, *he* will be the one to survive this. God always seems to give idiots the help they need.

6.

"**M**uthafuckas ain't tellin' if they know who it was," Meechie says, sounding out of breath, as you close the screen behind him. "I asked all over the place."

"So you think it might be somebody you know?" you ask.

"Maybe," he says. "But prolly not," he murmurs. "I mean, who the fuck kills anybody over weed? And from what the paper say, they didn't touch any of the product."

It turns out that the fire made the news, which is good because the media can fill in some of the blanks on what the cops know. Since most of the weed was kept in the fridge, it was still there when the cops finally got to it. But there's no mention of your cousin's name, or his mother's. And there's no mention of Alonzo or his body. So whoever was there covered up the worst of the charges. So much for finding a gun. Even so, there's no doubt that your boy is a dead man. If he wasn't he would've checked in by now. Duronté, however, is wanted for questioning, which means you were at least right about one thing.

Normally these kind of things happen over real estate. Maybe word got out that your cousin was coming up in the world and they figured the best thing to do was take him down a notch, show him that it's real in the battlefield and all that. This is the kind of thing the person who did it would keep his mouth open wide about, knowing that it would either draw out his enemies so that he could get a clean shot, or that it would prove Duronté didn't have the nuts to do anything about it.

Either way, you're not so sure of where to begin, and you can't trust any of the people you've got on the street past doing what they already do. Shit, you've only been up and running for a matter of days now. There's no telling what kinds of rats and snitches might be on the payroll. Duronté threw a lot of money into the furnace that was supposed to fuel the engine to carry you to *Lifestyles of the Rich and Famous* status. But right now all you've got are dead bodies with the threat of even more. Sound familiar?

You and Meechie sit there for what seems like hours but is really only about half of one, trying to figure out how to bring the niggas who got Alonzo back into the open. This ain't TV, so you know that any pros won't make the simple mistake of putting themselves in your sights. They'll be ordering takeout and staying low for a while. And if they came from out of town, they're already gone.

The practical thing is to let it go, but if word gets out on the street this early that y'all are weak, plenty of somebodies will do their best to body the anybodies in your crew as soon as possible. Yet you don't have the manpower for a full-fledged war. You're also trying to wrap this up with a bow. There's still school, after all. You tell Meechie that you'll call him if you need him. But for now you've got to think. It's just before 4. Duronté should be trying to hock his ride somewhere in Birmingham.

You realize that there would have been no less risk in him driving straight there. But he had said that he was "tired of that piece a shit anyway." You found it hard to believe when you heard the words. You thought that car was his pride and joy, the one thing God had given him, if nothing else, with that lottery ticket.

You drive to the Ikea in the city and drop close to two grand on furniture. You don't really even look at what color things are. You just want to fill the space, to give your mind something to do while you try and figure out where you are and what moves you have to make on a board where the enemy has taken far more from you than you have from them.

You jam more boxes than you thought could ever fit into a CRX and wheel them back to your place. You're assembling your futon when the phone rings. It's Frank.

"We need to talk," are his first words.

"About what?" you ask, keeping it cool, playing it like nothing he tells you can matter.

"My bad about yesterday," he says humbly. "I ain't mean to try you like that. Lonzo was my man. I known D and Jamar forever. And you was there, this outside nigga from New York callin' the shots, and I took it personal."

"Ain't no room for personal in business," you say.

"I know who hit Lonzo!" he blurts out.

"Who?" you ask coldly.

"Them niggas from Chicago."

"Which niggas from Chicago?"

"The ones you buyin' from. They ain't no suppliers. They fuckin' killas. I done jobs wit' them before. They workin' for somebody."

"And how come you just tellin' me this now?"

"'Cuz I ain't know about it until right now. Ran into my man in the emergency room and he told me a piece. Once you got one piece, the others come to you, if you know what I mean. That's why I said that we need to talk."

Part of you thinks that this is the kind of break you were hoping for, something to come aloose on its own. But you can't be sure if you should trust Frank. How can you trust anyone whose ass you kicked the night before?

"So whatchu want me to do?" you ask.

"You ain't gotta do shit. I'll put the work in myself. The only time you hear about it is when they set the wake."

"How do I know if this shit ain't a setup?"

"You can come with me if you want. Put somebody behind my seat with a fuckin' pistol. I got three cracked ribs and a dislocated shoulder. Good thing it ain't my shootin' arm."

"We are on the phone, you know. Meet me on Old National."

There's a short pause.

"What time?"

"Let's say 8," you reply. That is four hours away. Jamar should be out of Drama Club way before then.

"A'ight," he says, hanging up the phone.

You don't know what scares you more, the prospect of having to kill somebody tonight or the idea of walking into the setup of all setups and dying over some shit just because you were a guest in the wrong house during the wrong week. You think about Jennifer, even though you can't afford to. You need a bigger piece of the God-given magic that is her body. But not now.

That Glock of yours still hasn't been fired. While you want it to stay that way, you'll feel safer if it's under your seat. Your tags are in-state, and from now on you'll stay in the right lane and under the speed limit. No more weed. No more drinking in the ride. Keep the volume on your system low. Make yourself invisible to the all-seeing eyes and you'll get there without any surprise stops. You have to keep moving. That's the only thing left to do.

"So what you mean you used to work for him?" you ask Frank as you hand him a taco from the value pack you just picked up. You've been across the street from the Dugan's parking lot for an hour. You can smell the wings from outside.

"I did my last bid in Chi'. Boosted a van for some dudes that wanted to hit this jewelry store. Shipment was coming in and they had one of the guards ready to throw a wrench into the routine so that they could make the grab. Somebody fucked up and the two dudes never made it to the car. They went out the back and I pulled off just before the cops got there. Weeks of fuckin' planning and they still didn't get it right. But they got outta there like ghosts. One minute they were all over the police scanner, the next minute the cops is scratchin' they heads. Shit was like seven years ago but I remember it plain as day. Cops caught me right out front. I was singin' to Cameo's 'Single Life' on the radio when the cop came and tapped on the glass. And that was fuckin' that. So I'm here at the Flame the other day with my boy Terry and we see one of 'em, Larry, you know the lighter-skinned one"—he means Almond. "Dude is buyin' me drinks and tellin' me to stay around and kick it with him."

"And did you?" you ask.

"Hell yeah, I did!" he grins. "How the fuck was I supposed to turn down free drinks and dances?"

He goes on to explain that the next thing he knows, he and Almond are the best of friends. You wonder why anyone rolling in a Beemer like his is going to the Flame instead of Magic City, but maybe he's into the occasional chick with stretch marks and the one who calls every man gay who doesn't want a dance from her skinny ass.

Somewhere over the course of the night, Frank lets it slip that he's working for somebody now, someone who's making a lot of moves in a lot of different places. At first you wonder if Star isn't dead after all, if the whole car crash thing up in New York was just cover-up so that he could go underground.

But that kind of shit doesn't happen in real life, and even if it did, wouldn't you be more than enough of a reason for him to show up and pull the trigger himself? And why the fuck would anyone have a guy playing top dog in an out-of-town operation who can't keep his mouth shut?

But Frank's encounter with Almond had taken place the day before the twins paid Jamar that visit. And as Duronté wasn't into anything heavy, maybe they threw caution to the wind. You want to be that lucky for once.

So now you're parked diagonally across from the club. The Beemer's in the valet part of the lot so you know he's back in there. Hell, maybe both of them are. If they come out, you'll follow them wherever they head and start shooting until you get some answers. But you have to find out if Frank's story is real or not while still trusting in his plan. It's going to be a balancing act. But at this point, it's the only thing that makes sense.

You sit out there for the better part of three hours, taking turns resting your eyes. There's nothing but the sound of crickets and valet parkers talking shit about which dancers they're sure they can fuck. What are the chances of a couple of dudes getting paid to park people's cars getting with women who find new suckers every month to pay their rent? It's like going up against an army with a pistol. But ego gets everybody's ass in a sling at least once.

Part of you wants to go inside and see the sights. But the rest of you knows that if anybody in there recognizes you, it's all over. Either they call in the dogs and you walk out of the club to catch a drive-by, or they turn tail and disappear, leaving your enemy without a face. And if you don't have faces or names, you're gonna be up shit's creek real fast.

"You done this kinda shit before?" you ask Frank.

"I done every kinda shit there is to do," he says with a sigh. "This shit right heah ain't gonna be no biggie."

"I thought you said you was cool with this dude."

"I worked with him *once*. And I ended up doing five because of it. Did them muthafuckas keep my commissary phat? Did they take care of my kids? They ain't do shit but keep breathin'. So why the fuck would I stay loyal to 'em?"

You give him a nod. It sounds reasonable enough. And though you ain't a career criminal, you can say that it actually sounds fair. There ain't no honor among thieves or any of that shit. Will taught you that much.

Forty-five minutes later, Almond comes out of the place in the same suit you last saw him. He looks so full of liquor that he might bleed it if you cut him. There a broad with him: light-skinned and skinny. No tits. No ass. All legs. But if that's his thing, so be it.

He hands her the keys and she drives them out of the lot. You wait til they turn at the light and then follow them onto 285 going south. They turn off on the Campbellton Road exit heading over to 85, where they turn north into midtown. They park at the Sheraton Colony Square. But you still have to park, which means you might lose them.

"I should try and see what floor they're going to," you say.

"You don't have to," Frank replies with a grin.

"Why?"

"Because he already gave me the room number. The muthafucka might've told me where he kept the weight if I had asked. He was that gone."

"He usually hold?" you ask, worrying that your two guns might not be enough.

"Prolly. But I ain't never seen him pull out. He's supposed to be a killer and all that, so I cain't really say."

This crime is definitely more of an art than a science. Or at least it seems to be with the clowns you're working with. You both get out of the car with your pieces, yours at the back of your jeans with a shirt as cover, his lodged between jeans and his hip bone. Your breathing gets heavy—it's only a matter of minutes before you're back in the bottom of the hell you just escaped from. That boomerang is coming right back for you. You can feel it cutting through the air, calling your name. You almost want to just stand there and wait. You almost want it to put you out of your misery.

7.

You notice that there's a full moon as you cross the street to the hotel entrance. A warm breeze is in the air, and for once the night isn't trying to strangle you with humidity. This is the kind of night where you should call up a broad and watch movies on her couch. You even have a number to dial for once. But instead, you've got the barrel of a pistol rubbing against your ass cheek, and before the night is over you just might have to kill somebody.

Frank pops a stick of Trident in his mouth and starts humming Mobb Deep's "Shook Ones Pt. II," mouthing the lyrics as a piano lounge fills with folks who will never have a clue. The guy at the piano reminds you of Magnum P.I.

Instead of catching the show, you both cut left for the elevator banks. The hotel concierge gives you a nervous look, but it doesn't last long. She probably figures you're a rap group—she must see a few of them. You'd like to see more of the legs underneath that skirt. You wonder if her pussy hair is as blond as the mane on her head. But unfortunately there's no time or means to find out.

"Hit 23," Frank says. You follow his order. The doors close.

"You ever been in this hotel before?"

"Yeah, I think so," he says, biting into his gum like it's *carne asada*.

"What's security like?"

He shrugs his shoulders. "They ain't gonna stop Ocean's 11. I'll put it to you that way."

You're wondering if there are cameras in the elevators and hallways, if you'll get picked up on tape coming and going from the room. You're on 17 when your spider-sense goes off. You turn to Frank just in time to see him reaching for his piece.

His nose isn't taped across the middle, so you realize that you didn't actually break it. But it shows red on his caramel. You fire a jab at his nose, but he moves and somehow you end up hitting him in the throat. He starts to cough as he loses his grip on his pistol.

You aim to kick him in the nuts, but he catches your angle and slams you against the elevator, trying to pin your wrists with one hand. Your knee to the groin is on target and he doubles over. You kick him in the face, pull your own piece, and fire a single bullet. The round peels a piece of his forehead off like a scab. He falls to the elevator floor, dead.

The doors open at 23 just as blood starts to

pour from the hole in Frank's head. You back out, not knowing who's in the hallway. You check your clothes. No blood you can see. Most of it's splattered against the elevator wall. There's sixteen left in the clip, plenty of ammo to get some answers with. There's just one problem. He didn't tell you the room number before you killed him. You're praying there are no cameras.

Since you're not going to go door-to-door with a body in the elevator, you have to make a run for it. Once that elevator returns to the lobby, somebody's going to call the cops. Once somebody calls the cops, you've got five minutes to get out of there before you face the risk of some full-scale building search that's going to get you at least ten for manslaughter. Fuck that.

You head for the closest stairwell and track down twenty-three flights. You jump the last step on every floor, trying to pick up speed, trying to get to the building exit before somebody spots the body. You can feel the sweat staining your pits as you push your body downwards. You get to the first floor just as the commotion starts brewing over by the elevator banks. You glide through the automatic doors and out to the street while guests and staff set their eyes on the man who just tried to kill you.

Two cop cruisers explode over the hill and right up to the hotel entrance. You turn the key in your ignition the minute they come to a stop and pull off into the night. You wonder if he sold you out because of the ass-whipping or if it had already happened before that.

Every nerve in your body begins to tremble as you turn onto Ponce de Leon and push north toward Briarcliff. You take in deep breaths. You try to remember everything in that book on meditation you once took out of the library. You picture yourself back at your crib, assembling all the furniture, putting things on the walls, flipping through school catalogs to nail down which classes you're going to take.

You think of calling Meechie, but what's he going to tell you? He and Jamar are looking to you as their interim leader. They're waiting for you to call the shots. But you don't exactly know what you're supposed to do. Your lucky break almost turned into a romantic getaway to some drawer in the coroner's office.

You pull into Dugan's, which is still open and packed. Boys and girls playing the "game" game. You order three shots of tequila, a Corona, and a basket of hot wings. The bartender announces last call. You avoid the clock, afraid of what time it is. You haven't slept in two days now. It's all starting to wear on you.

There's a tall girl with skin the color of milk chocolate who keeps looking over at you. She plays with her fries, whirling them in the air between her thumb and index finger. But just as you think of saying something, her man, some Michael Vick reject without the canine problem takes her by the arm and leads her out, most likely so that he can spend the next few hours rearranging her vertebrae. Some dudes have all the luck.

The liquor winds you down far enough to get a handle on things. You'll have to dump that Glock someplace where it'll take weeks for it to wash up. And you need to dump it soon. Frank will be all over the news by morning and the Chicago twins must already know that you're onto them. They probably think Frank told you more than he did. That's a card you'll need to play a little closer to the finish line.

You make your way out of the bar and across the parking lot. There's an old train bridge running behind an apartment complex. You scale a deep hill and wander around in the darkness. You pass a group of homeless men playing chess with flashlights so that they can see the board. There's a junkie shooting up off to the side. You come upon a huge pit filled with nothing but old bottles, cans, and trash floating in about four inches of stale water.

You wipe the gun down and toss it into the pit. Any descriptions the concierge or other witnesses provide will be vague. You didn't park in the garage so there's no footage of you coming or leaving. Or maybe there is. According to the hunch that just started forming in your head, it may not matter either way.

You don't know where to go from the Dugan's lot. It feels like the sun will be up soon. You should go home and sleep. But you're not really sure if your house is even safe. For all you know, Frank has told them everything. You still can't figure out what it is they want. This can't be just about Duronté. If it was, they wouldn't have gone after *you*. But it can't be about you either. No one knows you here. This is the place you came to for a clean slate.

You think back through everything you've done since you arrived. It all started with Duronté, the night you went with him to sell that weed and found bodies in a dumpster. Alonzo died two nights later. The next day, Frank tries to whack you in a hotel elevator.

You take 20 to the AUC exit and cut down to Ashby and then past the block where Duronté's crib is nothing but rubble and ash. You just hope that she's awake. You hope that she'll let you in.

"You want some?" she asks, offering you what's left of her joint.

"Nah, can't fuck with that just now."

"And why's that?" she asks.

"I need all my brain cells."

"Oh, so it's thinkin' cap time?"

"Sumthin' like that."

"And what you thinkin' about?" She runs her nails along your scalp. It tickles.

"Business I gotta handle."

"Good or bad?"

"Getting badder by the minute," you say.

She thinks on this for a moment, as if you've told her your problems in full, as if she could possibly understand what you're caught in the middle of. You kiss her and she gives you her full lips to play with. Her hands stroke you through your jeans. You want to use your erection to explore the places she only let you touch with your fingers on date number one.

"You want my pussy?" she asks, pulling her Akademiks T-shirt up over her head. Her bra is the prettiest shade of purple, and it slides down to reveal big areolas with thick nipples to match. You bring your mouth down to them, sucking like they hold your last meal.

You run your fingers up the inside of her thighs, spreading them open. You can feel the heat coming from her pussy. No panties. Her shorts are already on the floor. You're pulling down your jeans when she starts playing with your zipper. The next thing you know, she's reaching inside. Then she's bringing you to her lips, taking you into her mouth.

You thicken and lengthen as she places the condom between your fingers. You roll it on and push slowly into her moist slit, feeling it throb all around you. Each thrust is like falling into heaven as she clamps her thighs around your waist.

She begins sucking on your neck and you forget all about Frank. You smell perfume and oil sheen and pussy all at once. She's so wet that your balls splash against her as you hit it from the back, sliding in and out, wishing that you could live in this place forever.

Your nut comes out of nowhere, a bigger one than when you came in her mouth the last time. You roll off her and onto the couch, where you try and catch your breath. Next thing you know, you're looking at the backs of your eyelids and then what's beyond. How the fuck did this day go to hell? There's an answer somewhere inside yourself. But you don't stay conscious long enough to find it.

You wake up alone on the couch, the room lit only by the bulb from the small fish tank in the corner. You don't know who she lives with or what she does. But Jenny makes you feel normal, that kind of normal you came here to find. You wish you had the time and the space to tell her. But right now those are luxuries you can't afford.

You lock the bottom lock on the front door as

you head out to your car. The sun is coming up outside and birds are singing those numbers they only do at the beginning of each day. Your tank is almost on E, so you head up the hill to the Amoco for gas, orange juice, and the *Atlanta Journal-Constitution*.

There's a picture of Frank on the front page. It looks like a mugshot. According to the article, they're looking for a black male of about your height and build. But there are no other distinguishing features—no name, no face for the APD to make you with. You are luckier than you thought.

The cops will be all over Frank's hood asking question that the locals won't be able to answer. After that, the cops will have nowhere to go and Frank's sheet will mostly speak for itself, an open file the boys in dark blue can probably live with. The trail will go cold and that will be all. But now *you* still have to make it make sense.

So how do you find the man who must now know you're looking for him? And even if you do find him, are you supposed to just ask him to sit down for coffee and that will be that? Hell nah. But you can't cap him either, because then you couldn't see who's at the top of this crazy pyramid. If you pull a trigger two more times, there's no way to find your truth. You become a loose end living on borrowed time by default.

The solution requires that you get lucky one more time, that you find the twins and follow them to someplace where you can control all the variables, where you can corner them and make them talk. Once you have a face, you'll know where you *can't* go. Once you see your enemy, you can figure out how to disappear . . . again.

You want to cry out that none of this shit is fair. But you already said it yourself: Taking lives will have God throwing everything but the kitchen sink in your direction. You just hope that you can dodge most of it.

You barely have the strength to pull the emergency brake when you park in front of your crib. It's even harder to get your key in the lock. It feels like you're carrying Frank on your back with the bodies from the dumpster tied to both of your legs. How come you have to take this weight all on your own? How come there's never another person with an ounce of fucking sense to help you figure it out? You guess that it's just not your lot in this life.

You'll have to be careful. You'll have to watch your step. No mistakes. But most importantly, you really have to get more sleep.

8.

You have a dream about running through the woods. Something's chasing you but you can't see what it is. You just know that it's moving faster than you, coming up on your tail. Your feet slow beneath you no matter how much you urge them to keep moving. Whatever it is, you can't get away from it. Whatever it is, you're going to have to face it.

You hear someone coughing on the other side of your eyelids and you pop them open. There are at least ten men surrounding your bed. The twins are standing right there, this time dressed in Adidas tracksuits instead of business attire.

"You sleep well?" Darker asks.

You don't answer. A small part of you holds onto the idea that this is a dream. The rest of you wants to slap your own face for laying your head in a place this obvious. Your only gun is back in that hole by the train tracks in midtown. You're fucked.

"Killin' a nigga can take a whole lot outta ya," Almond laughs. You imagine shooting his lips off and the kind of blood it would bring forth. It makes you smile, but a smile isn't good in this situation.

Somebody hits you with a hard left that nearly takes your head off.

"This isn't funny," Darker adds. "This is serious business."

If they were going to kill you, there wouldn't be this much talking. If they wanted to know something, they'd start asking. Right now they just want to scare, just want to make you feel like they have you in check. As you lay there in boxers without a real weapon in sight, you accept the fact that they're doing a pretty good job.

"I mean, on one hand, we gotta respect your gangsta," Almond says. "You caught Frank slippin', and that ain't some easy shit to do. Beatin' the piss out of him might have had somethin' to do with it, but that gets you bonus points with us. It says you ain't fulla shit like the rest of that crew you with. Duronté runs out of town right after we bring him in. Your boy Alonzo tries to pull out on us when we just wanted to ask some questions. He ain't leave us no choice."

"But why the fuck did you put him on in the first place?" you ask. "How come you ain't just do us that first night at D's crib?"

"Because it ain't on us. We got somebody to answer to."

"Who?"

"That ain't for you to know," Almond says.

You take a moment to scan the faces of all the men and boys surrounding you. Most of them are barely old enough to vote, much less drink. You ask yourself what it takes to get people to follow you. It's not your rep. It's not even your brains. It's having the power to make them think you know something that they don't. They're not here to kill you. They're here to ask you to join the team.

"What you gotta know is that the boss is impressed with you, that he wants you to take over for your cousin, even though you already been doing it. Now you got the power on your real estate. Now you get to play by your own rules."

"What if I ain't interested?" you ask.

"Then you go on permanent bed rest," one of the henchman in the background says, his hat pulled down so far over his eyes that he looks silly.

"It sounds like I don't have much of a choice," you say.

Darker smiles. "You don't. Pick up that work and get it out on the street. Your cousin's boys don't need to know about the change in management."

You nod, proof that you've got no secret plans to rock the boat, or at least none that they know about.

There's a long silence, as if everybody is processing what's just happened. You let the moment linger. You're not going to show them any cards that you don't have to.

"I need to know how to reach you."

"We already put the number in your phone," Almond says. "You need re-ups, you dial the digits. Anything else, you're on your own."

"Split the same?"

"Split's the name," both twins say in unison.

"Then I guess I better get to work."

"You should," Almond says as he starts toward the door. Most of the crew follows him, but Darker stays behind, most likely to bring up the rear.

"I got one question for you," you say to Darker. "Ask the boss why he picked me."

He smiles, obviously knowing something you don't. "So you know who you are and who you ain't."

Those words stay with you long after the crew is gone. As long as you stay in bed, you can still dismiss this as a dream, some figment of your imagination. Somebody's trying to make you sell their product. It reminds you of Snoop's verse on "Deep Cover." Except you couldn't pop eleven men at one time without ending up looking like a screen door. All of this and you don't really even have product out on the street.

You call Meechie, who you have call Jamar. You tell them to pick up the product. With so much up in the air, it looks like you might have to do the bagging yourself.

It's rush hour when Meechie and Jamar meet you at your crib. By then you have the dining room table and two chairs hooked up. The good thing is that you only have to bag it, that if Jamar's boy did it right you've got street-ready product and no more hassles, or at least not as many as there could be. Your little operation is waiting to get under way.

Even with three people, however, it seems to take hours. In the movies there are always people to do this shit for you, ones with the shower caps and masks and all that. But you ain't runnin' no Carter. In truth, what you have is a third-rate slacker operation. You had to kill your main muscle man (something you have yet to explain to your boys here), so if shit jumps off there's no one to protect you but you.

That bag of pistols at the car wash isn't going to be enough for the long run. If you make a dent with this thing, you've got to deal with everything from cops to jackers to snitches to rival dealers who don't wanna share their cake with nobody. It's like it only gets bigger. The hole only gets deeper, no matter how smart you are, no matter how good a plan you put together. They call it the *trap* because there are only two ways out, and neither of them are anywhere near as live as they sound in the songs on the radio.

It's kissing midnight when you're finally done. You break up the goods into loads for all of your different outlets and put them in Meechie's trunk, packed into gym bags with the product surrounded by 99-cent T-shirts, a good enough camouflage at first glance. They'll make the drops. You, on the other hand, have a very different assignment.

You would be a fool to blindly go to work for men you don't know, especially men who have been two steps ahead of you since this whole thing started. It just doesn't make sense from a business standpoint to unload that kind of coke to some newcomers and then whack the head of the household. They kill Alonzo and then send Frank to kill you. But why? You're fucking amateurs after all.

You drive out to the car wash and grab the bag of guns. You pick out the Sig Sauer P226 for yourself. Everything else goes in the trunk. After you lock up, you sit in the darkness of the car wash parking lot trying to figure out what your next move is going to be.

Your only shot is to try to find the twins again, on their own. You can't be sure if your stakeout with Frank was a planned thing, but you can imagine that ballers like these dudes love to blow dough to have some ass shaking in front of them. And there's a car you remember, a car that not just everybody has. Cruising the local gentlemen's clubs is a good start.

You've only been here a matter of days and yet you already know the main spots like the back of your hand. The D-boys own Magic City. On the weekend you can barely get a dance since they keep the best girls in the VIP, the best ass to themselves all night long. But if Almond is at the Flame, he's a cheapskate or a baller on a budget, which means you have to think smaller, more frugal, more average Joe.

Shooter Alley is way out in Doraville, a little off-the-beaten-path from where your boys have generally been moving. There's Pleasers and Body Tap and places far more grimy, places where fourteen-year-olds take the stage like it's a high school talent show. But this isn't their speed. The car says that they're into the finer things, or at least just fine enough. Mid-shelf broads for mid-shelf prices.

You travel from club to club, checking the parking lots and then going inside to try and match some familiar faces. You wear your cap low and one of the shirts you just bought from the mall, as all your clothes burned up with Duronté's.

At Pleasers you buy three songs from a tall chocolate thing with big eyes and a weave down her back. Large nipples on flat, floppy breasts. She could be in her mid-thirties but the ass has been preserved perfectly. No stretch marks, no cellulite. She grinds her ass into you, searching for the erection she knows is there. She teases it with thighs she moves back and forth between your legs. Then she grinds again, making you so hard that you're throbbing. She makes you want to buy her for the night but you resist the temptation. You're there on business after all. Another shot of Corzo later and you're back on the move.

Shooter Alley is surprisingly empty for this time of week. All colors of ass are united in the pursuit of pleasure and the patrons' money.

"What you doin' up in heah?" a fine-ass Asian girls asks, the curves in her legs sharp enough to split a hair in half.

"Lookin' for you."

She leads you to a chair where she jumps into a handstand that puts her top on bottom and her bottom on top. Her crystal-blue heels are above your head as she winds her body in front of you. The muscles in her arms don't show how much of an effort they're making. But it is when she spreads her legs that you see the true prize. And it's not the one between her thighs. Darker has just taken a seat at the bar.

You weren't expecting to see the other twin at a joint like this. Hell, for all you know they could really be twin brothers, subject to the same tendencies, attractions, or even addictions. And while his lighter-skinned brother prefers the Flame, he's way the fuck out here, drinking MGD and flirting with some blonde who has the worst tit job since Dominique Simone's.

Darker caresses the broad's all-but-bare ass as she stands next to him at the bar. He listens to what she says like it really matters. She brushes the back of his perfectly cropped Caesar the way a woman does to her man. This is why you didn't see him out at the club. He was at a different club with some blonde who'd probably rather not be down in the SWATS. Once again, the Good Lord has given you quite a break.

As he's just gotten here, you know that he's going to stay for a while. Get a few dances, maybe even a quick blowjob in the VIP room. Then he's going to take her back to wherever he's laying his head. With any luck, they'll be going it completely alone, so caught up in their romance that they won't see you coming.

You switch over to club soda but you keep buying dances. You've still got plenty of money so you're okay. Besides, ten bucks a dance isn't going to kill you. You spend enough money where the girls finally start to ask your name. They want to know where you're from and how come they haven't seen you before.

You tell them that you're from D.C. and that you're down here on business. You're the sales manager for an office supply chain store that's just moving into the area. Lisa, a Salvadoran with a g-string on her perfectly round ass, asks you if you have a girl.

"Why you askin'?" you reply, happy that you cut off the tequila, because the buzz is coming in like strangers when you leave the door open.

She looks you up and down. "'Cuz I'll give you pretty babies, *papi*," she says seductively.

You're seriously considering taking her up on her implied offer when you see your boy and the blonde making their way out on the other side of the crowded room. You tell the broad that you're going to take a piss, but you head for the door instead, maybe thirty paces behind them.

She's driving a fuchsia Honda Accord with chrome factory rims. It looks very trailer trash, very cheesy. But what do you expect? She's a fuckin' stripper.

You follow them back into the city to the IHOP in midtown. The broad puts away pancakes like they're going out of style. You can see through the window that all he's having is coffee.

From there, it's to an apartment complex in Buckhead. You consider going in all alone, but then you think better. Meechie's just a phone call away.

9.

You've been there close to an hour when Meechie and Jamar pull into the lot. Both of them look beat. But why shouldn't they, it's pushing 3 in the morning.

"So these niggas fuck while we out there grindin'?" Jamar asks from the backseat of Meechie's brand-new ride, a champagne-colored Yukon with tinted windows.

"The nigga above them probably just fuck at his crib. They prolly have pussy flown in for his ass."

They both laugh.

"Prolly ain't far from the truth," you say.

You have explained everything to them, not just because you don't want to keep them in the dark, but so they'll understand just how fucked they are with or without you. Not only have you all gotten played, but they're trying to make you turn the product around just *because*. Meechie and Jamar are just as angry and confused as you are. But they agree that you're right.

"So what's the plan?" Jamar asks.

You reach into the backpack and pull out the chrome .380.

"You stay in the car and wait with the engine runnin'. If somethin' goes wrong, you either wheel us out of here or break out. Somebody tries to jack you for the ride, you shoot 'em."

You doubt if there's going to be any gunplay in this part of town. It's quiet, relatively wealthy, and rarely in the news. But if Darker isn't holding a piece, he's the dumbest muthafucka south of Charlotte.

You and Meechie cock your pistols and make your way across the parking lot to the unit entrance and climb the stairs to the third floor, where you saw them go in. The door reads, *415B*.

You can both hear the sounds of fucking from inside, male and female moans and the abuse a mattress is taking. If you had a lock pick kit you could ease right in. But you aren't a locksmith or a burglar.

Meechie puts his ear to the front door and starts to giggle.

"Ole boy sho' is fuckin' the shit outta her," he says with a smile.

"How we gon' get in?" you ask in a whisper.

"Way I see it, we gotta kick it down."

You can say that you've kicked a door in before, but you can't say that you've done it well. Plus, you're worried about the noise you're going to make. All it takes is one neighbor and three digits before the cops have themselves two niggas with guns in the wrong part of town.

"Wait here," you whisper to your lieutenant. "If somebody comes, head back to the truck."

He gives you a nod and you creep down the stairwell to the rear of the building, where you find that each unit has a small terrace at the back. If you can climb three stories without falling, you've got a much easier entrance.

The wood railing is made of long thin beams, perfect for grabbing onto. But you'll need a running start and a decent vertical to make the leap from the ground floor up to the first rail. You take a few steps back and then you charge, building momentum with each step.

You throw every muscle in your body into defying gravity and you get just high enough to reach the bottom rail. You grab on with the other hand and pull yourself onto the ledge of the terrace, making sure not to knock anything over, making sure not to breathe too loudly, your eyes checking each of the three windows leading to the first-floor apartment. Nothing stirs.

You climb your way up to the second floor and then to the third. By the time you get there, the sounds of intercourse have died down. The sliding terrace door is open, but the screen is locked. This is indeed a whole lot easier to handle.

You remove the Swiss Army knife you've had since the Boy Scouts and use the big blade to slowly cut a hole in the screen. Then you reach in, flip the lock, and slide the screen door open.

Even in darkness you can tell that the place is decorated well. There's a thirty-five-inch plasma mounted on the wall with two pairs of ballet slippers mounted on opposite ends. The coffee table is made of crystal. There are framed photographs of a middle-aged man and woman who are most likely her parents. They smile for the camera, holding hands. It's so syrupy sweet that you almost want to hurl.

The bedroom is at the rear of the apartment, so you creep across to the front door. You unlock it and open the door a crack. You can see Meechie on the other side looking off in some direction. Then you hear footsteps behind you.

You spin around to raise your piece but your arm collides with what looks like a golf club. Darker is naked but ready, and he swings the iron in every direction. You duck and dodge, dip and stumble, not knowing where the hell your gun went.

He catches you across the back and then the knees. He winds up to hit you straight in the head, but Meechie tackles him out of nowhere. They struggle, knocking into things and shattering others on the carpeted floor. First thing you do is close the door and lock it. The second thing you do, while Meechie tries to apply a weak-ass choke hold, is kick the dude straight in the face. He goes out like a light.

You fall to the floor next to both of them holding your injuries. The floor is soft enough to sleep on, so soft that you forget about the white broad in the bedroom who's probably calling the cops. You turn around to say something to Meechie, but he's gone. Now there's a ruckus in the other room.

"Shut the fuck up, bitch!" Meechie yells to what sounds like the rhythm of open-handed slaps. In sixty seconds, he drags her out like a calf tied up at some state fair, her wrists and ankles bound by a pair of dress belts. He flips a switch and the room floods with light. The glare stings your eyes.

You race past both of them without a word, acting faster than you can think, and dig through her chest of drawers. Naturally, the handcuffs are underneath three pairs of bloomers at the very back of her top drawer. You head back into the living room, cuff Darker's wrists behind his back, and tie his ankles with your own belt. Then you find your gun, which is poking out from under the couch, a long ways from where he batted it out of your hand.

Darker is bleeding at the temple when he comes to a few minutes later. "You must be here for something," he groans.

"We're here for *you*, baby," you say. "So who's the man?"

"What do you mean?" he asks, as if you said the words in another language.

"Who sent you here for us?"

He cracks a smile and an icy sensation runs through the length of your body. The truth is about to come out. But it may not be the truth you were expecting.

Meechie's looking at you and you're looking at him. But no one's watching the broad. Someone should be watching the broad.

"Why the fuck would anybody trust your stupid-ass cousin with that kind of product? I know you asked yourself the question."

"Yeah, I did."

"Somebody wants to remind you of who you are, no matter where you rest your head."

His eyes meet yours. The image you see has to be wrong. You have to be jumping to conclusions. A hammer hits a round in a chamber, sparking gunpowder, which in turn sends a bullet at a speed of 400 miles per hour for the five feet between the gun and the side of Meechie's head. It splatters into his skull and he falls to the floor, dead.

Instinctively you shoot her in the chest and immediately train the gun on Darker. The interrogation is over now that cops are presumably being called because of the sound of gunfire. But there's a new decision that must be made.

You only kill when you have to. This has been

a rule of yours every since shit got hectic. But now you're in a situation where you may need to kill a man who you don't have to. You need to, but you don't have to.

You don't have to look over at Meechie to know that he's dead, and you don't have to look at the broad to figure the same. Sure it was self-defense, but which way will your boy here spin it once the cops arrive? You can't implicate him without him doing the same to you.

He could easily get away with saying that you changed the crime scene to make it look like self-defense. Put one in his head and he can't tell the story. Make a quick run through the crib to see what you can grab. And then go out the terrace door, down the three stories, and make the hundred-yard dash back to either Jamar or to your own ride, dodging the cop cars all the while.

And if you leave him, you still won't get to heaven. You've gone too far and done too much.

You look him straight in the face as you put one between his eyes, petrifying him upon the moment of impact. You run to the back of the apartment, find his wallet, and are out the back door to the lawn underneath.

You can see Jamar in the Yukon across the lot just as the squad cars arrive with sirens blazing. You hide in the path of evergreen trees that separate the complex from the sidewalk. Then you call

Jamar on his cell and tell him to meet you in front of the Barnes & Noble just across the way.

You jaywalk across the nearly empty Peachtree Street and squeeze behind a column, out of view from any cops who might be coming from the complex. Jamar pulls up moments later. It occurs to you that you'll have to go back for your car or run the risk of getting it towed. But if they run the plates, you don't have a record. For all the cops know, you ran out of gas and went for help. Besides, as long as you dump the gun you should be good. Too bad this town doesn't have a river.

"Where you wanna go?" Jamar asks.

"Your house," you say.

You realize that you are running out of both homeboys and places to hide. Jamar begins to sob at the wheel, tears coming down his face one at a time, like a doll or an actor in a movie. You can't blame him though. He's seen two of his boys killed and another run out of town. It's down to you and him. The business is a joke. Your futures are a joke. Nothing matters until you finish this once and for all.

Jamar's house is a tiny two-bedroom apartment on Oglethorpe Street down by the train station. His father is a truck driver who is rarely home. His mother's doing five for possession with intent to distribute. A lot of the money Jamar makes goes into her commissary.

Someone has frozen a game of BioShock on the Xbox in the living room just before their character is about to be killed.

"My brother always leaves that shit on," Jamar complains as he locks the door behind you.

There are textbooks all over the ratty leopard-skin couch and the only picture on the wall shows a black Jesus, a painting you've seen somewhere before, probably in a pile on a roadside where some vendor was selling them. You've never understood how so many people could want to own the same picture, how so many people could want nothing more than to be like everyone else.

You've had Darker's wallet in your hand ever since you left the complex. But you've been afraid to open it. You've been saving it for a time and place where you could sit down and examine it.

You plop yourself on a floor that smells like soy sauce and cat piss, then flip the leather wallet open. In it you find an ATM card, a Blue Amex, and a non-driver's ID from the State of New York. Turns out that Darker was always being escorted because he isn't licensed to drive. Maybe he'll take the time to learn in his next life.

But it's the ID that comes with the biggest surprise of the early morning. Stephen Mackintosh. Mackintosh. That's Will's last name. And as you stare at the letters, you can see him mouthing those words about his cool-ass twin cousins (one dark and one darker) who he kicked it with on his one trip out of town, to Chicago, when he was fifteen. Will is who they were protecting. Will is the reason why there's nothing left of your cousin's crew but the high school kid.

All of this had been a message crafted carefully for you. He knew you wouldn't have voluntarily gone back into the game. He also knew that you would be tempted to play detective. He knew that you would kill if you had to. He knew that you didn't think he could reach that far, that he couldn't touch you from 900 miles away.

What he wants is for you to fulfill your obligations. What he wants is for you to come home.

Despite all your dreams of cake to go with your coffee, in the end there will be nothing. In days or hours, those working for you will be told that you're no longer in charge. Your brand of crack rock will come and go like a washed-up rapper's career. You are back at zero and a lot of people are dead . . . again . . . and all because of you. At least you kept the kid alive.

There never was a normal life for you, not at long as you had Will in your rearview, not as long as you refused to face the music from Tony Star's jukebox. You did what you were told, but you didn't end up dead as planned. The man who raised glasses with you wants your life to be over.

Maybe you've become a target for everything

you can't control. You are Moby Dick. You are Stringer Bell. You are Frank Lucas. Livin' ain't livin' until he's seen your corpse. So if you want to move on, you have to give it to him. But you ain't gonna make it easy. There's no way in hell you're going to make it easy.

10.

By the early afternoon, that white broad's apartment complex is completely cop-free. Your CRX doesn't have so much as a smudge on it. You take the bag you packed out of the back of Meechie's truck and load it into your own, right next to the sack of guns. You tell Jamar you'll be back as soon as you can. Interstate 85 will take you right to 95 North. Then it's a straight shot all the way up the coast.

You could've taken the train or the bus. Security checks on those are usually a joke, so the bag full of guns could just as easily be stuffed with candy as far as they're concerned. But you need the time to prepare yourself. You need the time to come up with a plan.

You can't get Meechie out of your head, the way that bullet took him out in less than a second, how he got killed by some white broad you had planned to let live. At least you didn't see Alonzo die. At least your cousin got away. At least you have some kind of consolation in the fact that the very plan seemed to be killing them off until you were the last left, until you were all alone again, just like it had been the last time.

But what was supposed to happen then? Were the twins going to throw you in some car trunk and take you back to Brooklyn? Will must have an outstanding warrant, so he can't fly anywhere. Maybe he was planning to have one of his crew drive him to some midpoint, where he'd break it all down like some B-movie bad guy. He would look you in the eye and tell you why. But you already know why.

When it all comes down to it, you were Abel to his Cain. Even when you were dirty, they treated you like you were clean. It had been brewing for so long that it had naturally woven its way into Will's plans for takeover. He had to get to you as a part of rebuilding himself.

But that's not really the way you should be thinking about it. Based on what you know now, you're a dead man the minute you cross the bridge. Or at least he'll want you to be. But with one of his cousins down and the red tape of the APD, it could be weeks before they get a positive ID on Darker's body, unless he had a record. Even then, it should still take at least a little while to run him through the criminal database, hopefully long enough for you to get to Will, even though that's the hardest part of your new situation.

If he can reach you this quickly in Atlanta, he's most likely sitting pretty in New York. Plenty of

men. Plenty of money and eyes covering every inch
of ground he has to roll across. You, on the other
hand, have no one—no one to call, no one to help
you in any way, not even a place to lay your head
anymore. There's about ten grand in that savings
account you left behind, but you don't think you're
going to need it. If you do this well enough, you
won't even have time to make the withdrawal.

The first thing is to find somewhere to rest,
somewhere cheap, somewhere below the radar.
You think about trying to track down your Rover,
the one that's probably riding it out in an impound
lot, but once again you don't have the time for that
kind of luxury. You'll have to deal with cabs and
a motel somewhere outside of the neighborhood,
maybe one of those Russian joints down in Brigh-
ton Beach.

All of these things matter, as you're outnum-
bered and outgunned. Whether you fail or make it
happen, you'll still be on the run. A dead man near
the top sends shockwaves through everything. It
takes food out of kids' mouths. It turns corners
against one another.

You refill the tank in Greensboro just in time
to see some state troopers breaking up a dispute
between a guy and a pair of white broads. There
are TV cameras and a couple of men who look like
bouncers. You even make out the nerdy guy with
glasses. They're filming an episode of *Cheaters*,

which means that somebody just got caught stepping out on somebody else. You don't stick around to see which is which and what is what.

You're just past D.C. when your eyelids start closing against your orders. As you don't want to run into a semi, you pull into a motel and book a room for the night. Unlike that fleabag you visited to meet up with Reggie, this place smells like perfumed soap. The bed is already turned down. There isn't a trace of dust anywhere. As soon as you've given the room a once-over, you're laying under the crisp sheets, too tired to even turn the lights off.

Behind your eyes you see the old neighborhood, the way it was before all of this. You see the fat Yemeni with the Afro who flirts with all the young girls. You miss the salmon and mac-and-cheese at Exquisite. You miss Chief. You even miss Will. You remember that time he tried to pop a wheelie with his chair and flipped over. It was the funniest shit you'd seen in the world. Even Will laughed. It's the last time you remember all three of you laughing together.

Your eyes pop open nearly ten hours later. The sunlight at the edges of the closed blinds looks like fire at first glance. But after a few seconds you realize it's just another day. As this is your third day without a shower and checkout is in less than forty minutes, you jump at the opportunity.

You feel like a new man as the warm water covers you, followed by layers of lather and a fresh shave. You put on the second of your three new shirts, the green one with *Adidas* in black letters across the front, and a fresh pair of jeans. The clutch has left a scuff on your new Jordans. But it won't matter anyway since you've been voted Most Likely to Get Killed in Them.

You grab pancakes at the diner a few blocks up. It's owned by a guy named Mel and the cashier's name is Vera. Where the fuck are Flo and Alice? The coffee is like heaven though. It will definitely come in handy on your way to hell.

You don't really believe you're returning to the devil's playground until the skyline comes into view. You can remember being seven or eight down at the Brooklyn Heights promenade with your foster dad at night, trying to count the lights on in all the buildings. You asked him why people didn't turn them off when they left their offices and he explained that if they did, the world couldn't see New York. You asked why the world needed to see New York and he said something like, "Because this place gives more hope to the world than anywhere else."

Even as a kid you thought that he'd seen one

I *Love New York* commercial too many. But just like you, he had never lived anywhere else. He never knew what other cities might have been like. He died thinking that New York was the only place where he would ever belong. You felt the same way until you left. But now you're back, and you're probably going to die. So in the end you didn't get that much further than he did.

After the Holland Tunnel you go over the Manhattan Bridge into Brooklyn and hit a left on Myrtle. It's after lunch and before rush hour, so the traffic is relatively light. There seem to be more white folks on the streets than there were six months ago. More new buildings. Places that had been dead and buried for years have new windows and paint jobs. The windows have signs that say *Condo* and *Co-op* and *Commercial Space Available Here*.

The old corners are clean. There's a Subway sandwich shop where the old cleaners used to be. The pizza spot on Lafayette where you'd get chicken nuggets after school is now a donut shop promoting their newest blend of coffee.

But there's still the one-legged man in the *Puerto Rico* tank top rolling along Fulton. He's always thinking about his next drink, knowing that his disability check will be in the mail soon, and that the demons he seeks to escape are there waiting for his next bottle to run dry. You've read about alcohol being a killer, but this man's been at it for twenty years straight and he looks pretty much the same. From what you can tell, after losing the leg he's never been hurt again, never been sick, never missed a day on the avenue. He needs to be in the world in a way that Alonzo and Meechie and Star and all the others didn't. You have no idea why God does what he does. But then again, it's not your place to say.

Every few blocks you have to remind yourself that you shouldn't really talk to people. You're here to do a job that requires stealth. It's hard not to roll down the window and give a nod to the folks you know. So you push up Nostrand all the way out to King's Plaza.

You take a seat on a bench inside the mall and flip through a local newspaper, the *Brooklynite*. Somewhere in the classifieds you find an ad for rooms being rented weekly. The woman who answers the phone sounds Eastern European, maybe Serbian. She says there are openings at seventy dollars a week, which includes utilities and fresh sheets. Four people share a shower. You don't plan to be around long enough for that to get annoying.

It's about five minutes away from the mall. The woman from the phone is tall and slender. You can tell that when she was younger, her titties probably stood straight out, defying gravity. Now they sag. The circles under her eyes are dark. At some point she had been a contender, even if it was a lifetime earlier and in a place halfway around the world.

She leads you to the fourth room on the hall. There's a dingy window, a water stain on the ceiling, and a full-sized bed with a bent frame. You don't ask how the damage came about. You give her three Benjamins for a month's rent and a look that says she needs to beat it. She exits quickly, her aging pussy most likely moist from the smell of new money.

You sit your bags down and stretch out on the bed. Your feet dangle over the edge but it's softer than you ever would have imagined. Your eyes close and you sleep again. This time you see nothing but darkness. You float through that beautiful nothing for hours.

Your phone jerks you awake, the tone playing a snippet of Big Boi's "Kryptonite" until you answer. There's a voice on the other end of the line that you don't expect. It's Chief.

"You here yet, nigga?"

You don't say anything. This is a number he shouldn't have. But then again, you shouldn't be here in the first place. You pull yourself together and speak.

"How you know where I am?"

"You know the answer to that," he says. "We need to talk."

"What, before you put a hole in me?"

"You don't even know what's been goin' on."

"You can explain if you want."

"Not on the phone. Meet me down in Dumbo, on that little gravel part under the bridge. I'll be there by myself. This ain't a setup. I put that on everything."

"What time?"

"Two hours, like 11."

"I'll be there," you say, and then hang up.

You reach into the bag for the Beretta and the .380, the only guns still there. For some reason you thought there were more. Your legs start to tremble as you begin to think it all through. You're tired. You're worn down. You could stay here for a month and there's no way they'd find you. You could wait for the cops to get to Will and Chief and the rest of them, and everything would be fine. You don't have to meet Chief. You could even turn tail and head to Cali. You could stand by on the first flight out of JFK and never look back.

But you ran once already. And those you left behind are the ones who went after your new life the first chance they got. All of this sneaking around, all of these precautions, and they found you as easily as if you had a sign around your neck with your name and phone number painted on it. Duronté should never have trusted you. No one should have.

* * *

You haven't been downtown in a long time. You used to go to the movies on Court Street, but then you stopped. Maybe it was because you always ended up sitting in front of two people who didn't know how to keep their mouths shut while the picture was rolling. Maybe it was just easier to get whatever you wanted to see on bootleg for half the quality and half the price.

You park on Joralemon and make the walk down to Front and then all the way out to the meeting spot.

No one used to come down here when you were growing up. People would talk about it as a place where junkies would come to shoot up. Being high in front of the skyline gave their delusion an added effect. And when that delusion ended, they'd head back to civilization, past the Fort Greene projects, so that they could rob somebody else in the name of getting another delusion going.

You look around as you come closer to the spot. There are no parked cats with shadowy figures inside, no suspicious-looking people pretending to walk dogs or read newspapers at 11 o'clock at night. There is, however, a figure sitting on the stone steps that lead to a beach—a manmade stretch of rocks and gravel currently swallowed by the tide.

Thirty yards closer and you can see that it's

Chief. He's picked up about twenty pounds in six months and has one of those sculpted beards that the barbers darken. As you come up on him, he looks like the loneliest man in the world.

"If you gonna kill me, get it over with sooner than later," you say.

Chief turns to you with the smallest of smiles across his lips.

"What's so funny?" you ask, pushing more threat into your tone.

"I ain't never been no killer," he says. "If I was, I wouldn't need you."

"How'd you get my number?"

"You been livin' in the '90s," he says. "Everywhere that you used a debit card after you left, Will knows about. He got some private investigator keeping tabs on you like that."

This is the part when you feel really stupid. "So he knew I was comin'?"

"People been on the lookout for days. Somebody saw you in that sorry-ass Honda today and called me. I got your number off the computer at Will's crib."

"So what you want with me?"

"Nothing," he says, as if merely saying the words brings some kind of relief. "I just want all this to be over with."

11.

"Lookin' back, I knew from the beginning," Chief concludes.

Both guns are cold and heavy against your back. But you keep them right where they are. It has taken more than an hour for your boy to explain everything that has happened since you left. Very little of it surprises you at this stage. But when he's done, all the gaps are completely filled.

It turns out that Will let Star go only so that he could frame him for a murder. He got one of those guys who had actually survived the ambush to flip for him and testify that Star had killed Her. Neither Chief nor he know that you were the one who pulled the trigger on that one. Or maybe they do.

Their crew broke out as soon as the last man had fallen, leaving a body count in the double digits over the course of a day, including the ones you bodied. The story had gone national, but the murder couldn't be pinned on anybody. All the guns were found clean of prints. No witnesses. It was like the Terminator had come out of nowhere, whacked an entire crew, and then vanished.

On the underneath, Will sent people to all of Star's strongholds that he knew about. He sent them in suits, speaking in code, pretending to be liquor distributors, wannabe bouncers, or real estate agents.

But as it turned out, an army in the hands of that crazy nigga in the wheelchair was the absolute worst thing to happen. He turned into Hitler, making long lists of everyone still breathing who had done him wrong. He ran heists. He made hits. He set people up with the cops. He became that nerd that everybody shit on in high school back from the dead as a muscle-bound millionaire with a grudge to settle.

He scraped together the product that Star had left on the street while Star was making a run for the border. The package Will sent to the homicide detective on the falsified murder case got held in the mail for a few days, which had given Star a window to empty his vaults, transfer most of his money offshore, and make a run for it.

After that, whatever had been stretched thin inside of Will finally snapped. He invited the twins to Brooklyn to discuss the opportunity to set up their own franchise in the ATL. The catch was dealing with you. Will gave them the house address, information on Duronté, and whatever else he might have had. Then it was their show. Throwing away a low six figures in product didn't mean a damn thing to a wheelchair-bound maniac in over his head.

Then it all started to fall like dominos. Loyal crew members flipped like switches. Doors got kicked in. There were busts and seizures and more bodies. Chief didn't know why it hadn't made bigger headlines, but a cop in Will's pocket told them that the case was tied into a bigger DEA probe, that they wanted to hold out on making arrests until they had a lock on Will's supplier. But as the supplier vanished, so did their case.

Now there's no new product. Will's six-month rule is coming to an end. He's holed up like Nino Brown in a house off Ocean Avenue, trying to avoid the cops and find a new connect. But there's been no luck. He's made too many enemies and he doesn't have enough dudes left to hold out if there's a war.

"But what about me?" you ask.

"What do you mean what about you?" Chief replies.

"Why he so pressed to fuck my shit up?"

"He thinks all of it's your fault."

"The fuck is he talking about?"

"He said that you would have talked him out of the dumb shit he did that got him into this mess, that if he's about to go out, you should go out with him."

"Damn," you say. "He really is out of his mind!"

"C'mon, man, you know he ain't been right since Skate City."

There is a brief moment of silence when those words hit the air.

"He thought that if shit got hot down in ATL you'd come back, that you'd help him get shit right."

"That's what he said?"

"That's what he said."

"Then he really is crazy. How the fuck did the twins go along with this shit?"

"They ain't have a real choice," he replies. "You know how a crew works . . . So now you see why I called you down here."

"Yeah, but what do you want me to do about it?"

This is when he turns away from you, looking across the river toward where the Twin Towers used to be.

"Will has to go."

"Since when did I start being the man to put the work in."

"When you started puttin' work in," he says. "Star's bar, the dark-skinned fuckin' cousin, and his bitch. There was no way in hell you coulda got back here without bodyin' some muthafuckas."

"But what about you?" you charge back. "You been up here."

"Doin' what I always do," he replies smugly.

"Computers, Internet, cell phone. I'm the fuckin' nerd from the projects. I ain't around none of that. Shit, I'm lucky if Will even returns my phone calls these days."

What you want to know is why Will has to end up dead. You tell Chief that he can testify or find a way to frame Will.

"If he dies he comes back as someone else, somewhere else. He starts over, never remembering what he did here. Lock him up somewhere and he's trapped with his demons for another twenty years. I don't think he'd want that. All of this shit is about him not dyin' the last time."

When you think of your homeboy, you think of him still standing, of the three of you racing up the block, you and he neck-and-neck with Chief trailing behind, an ice cream bar in one hand and a pack of Now and Laters in the other. There was the arm-wrestling series, the professional league that gave you your first and only broken bone when you tried to hit Will with a flying elbow and ended up smashing your arm on the concrete.

You think about when you each kept count of how many girls did or didn't look you up and down in the hallways in middle school. You think about the twenty dollars riding on who would get some pussy first. You lost. And you paid. When he lost, he always made it playful, but underneath the fluffy words he was telling you to go fuck yourself. And you considered most of this when you left. Still, it hurts all over again.

But this isn't some storybook. It's not like you're carrying the only nine that can kill him or something. It's not like you don't have enough sins to try and balance out on judgment day. Yeah, you've killed, but you ain't that much of a killer.

"I can't even do it," you sigh. "You on your own."

Chief's face falls to the ground and shatters into a million pieces. He looks like a kid whose balloon is flying high into the sky and away from him forever. He wasn't expecting you to say no.

He parts his lips as if he's about to mutter something, words that never hit the air. The buckshot blows a hole in his back, spraying you with your homeboy's blood before he falls lifeless at your feet. You stare down at your fallen friend. From this angle he looks like just another dead body. And that's what you tell yourself. He's just another dead body, not another piece of the present made permanently past.

Chief's killer has a face that you recognize, one colored by grief and that same stupid grin he's been wearing since that first night you met him at Duronté's. Almond is here and now, and he's moved the next shell into the breech of his twelve gauge.

Your right hand is faster than your left, so it's the .380 you fire indiscriminately at the armed shadows coming toward you. This is a bold move, to let off like this in the middle of white-people land. But you like life. You like living. And as your last true friend in the world, who wasn't a killer but who just got killed, slips further into the darkness of departure, you want Will to know that you could've been a contender.

You once heard a line of dialogue in a movie that explained how every bullet has destiny, how each slug knows whether it will hit or miss. As you fire into the shadows, you witness blood exploding from their necks, arms, and torsos. They fire back, their rounds screaming past, missing by less than inches. It is as if you are being guided by some unknown force, as if you are being shielded from the rain of death heading your way.

Once, years ago, after both of you had gotten your asses kicked by some niggas from Hart Street, you and Chief stood before the small iron pot with the railroad spikes and machete in it that Chief stored in his room. He told you that an angel lived there, one who kept you out of accidents and made sure that you won fights. You remember standing there, dried blood on the sides of your busted lips, asking the angel in the pot to make you bulletproof. It seemed like such a far-fetched thing at the time. But now, as they fall, some probably dead and most wounded, you wonder if that prayer long ago was for this moment.

You don't check pulses. You don't kick guns away. You just run past them, over them, around them, moving as if they're still standing, as if they're still firing white-hot lead meant to take your life. You run in the direction they came from in hopes that there is someone waiting, someone in an idling vehicle left there to hit the gas once you and Chief are dead bodies.

And he is there, at the wheel. He can't see anyone coming back through the darkness. The side door is wide open. He doesn't see you until it's too late.

You keep your 9 at his neck as you have him drive you to where Will is. The driver is just a kid, maybe nineteen. Had this whole thing gone as it was supposed to, he could've bragged that he'd had a piece of the boss's big play for the night. Now he's just a terrified messenger.

You have him drive you to Flatbush, to that house off the park where Will's been holed up. All the lights are on. Silhouettes are moving behind closed curtains. Even if he doesn't know his boys had a bad day at the office, he's ready for the news. There's probably some dude with a Calico sitting by the front door waiting to spray half an army like roaches. Will probably has ten pistols taped to his chair. There's no way you're heading in there alone and coming back alive. But you will go in there. Not yet, but soon. And if you're going

to go out, you're going to take them with you—
finish the last chapter and close the whole book.
Amen and Amen. You have your boy drive to the
top of the park and then onto Fifth Avenue, oh so
far away from home.

You hit him in the face with the butt of your
pistol enough times to draw blood and knock him
unconscious. Then you leave him on a corner sidewalk to eventually get up and move on his way.
You never shoot the messenger. After all, you used
to be the messenger.

You drive the van all the way back to the board-
ing house, where you grab the bag that held the
guns. It still has an extra clip for your 9, as well as
a few other things you might need. You force yourself not to think about Chief. You force yourself
not to think about anything but the plan you're
writing page-by-page as you head back toward the
end of the line, the house with the moving silhouettes, the building where you will make your last
stand.

11.

Luckily for you the house is completely detached, one of those shacks they built for single families. You imagine that it probably belonged to some dead relative who left it to Will or to somebody else who he muscled it out from under. You park the van directly in front of the house and keep it running. The lights are still on but there are no more silhouettes in front.

You take a quick pass around the house. No guards. No cameras. It's a cakewalk for an ambush. But that whole army-of-one thing is bullshit. Yeah, you're gonna go in. But you ain't stupid either.

There's a ten-second delay on the grenade at the bottom of the bag. That's just enough time for you to jog up around to the side of the house, a spot where you have a perfect view of the door. Just the right angle. Just the right range.

The van goes up like a Roman candle, hot metal blowing out windows. Car alarms go off. The grass out front catches on fire. Your ears are ringing. But hearing is the last of your concerns. Three men spill out of the house looking like they just woke up. You don't think about their baby mamas or their kids. You don't think about how much they know about you. You just keep pulling the trigger until they fall, one flat on his face, another on his side, the third on his back with eyes looking up to heaven.

You wait for the cavalry to come, but nothing happens. You climb onto the small porch, reload, and creep up to the open doorway. You cross the threshold just as Will fires the sawed-off in his lap. He's been waiting for you. Only a few buckshots graze you, but they feel like hot knives tearing through your flesh. Your eyes tear.

You fire blindly, your legs kicking and scrambling like a bug turned on its back. He shoots again and you're covered in plaster. You crawl behind what you think is a couch. Seconds later you're tasting its stuffing when he lets off another round.

Someone else would spend this time taunting you. But Will doesn't underestimate you. He never has. The minute you stop breathing is the minute he feels safe, even if he'll never really be safe again. He fires once more and you hear the splintering of glass. A fire engine siren approaches in the distance. Then there's a click where another blast should be. He's out.

You jump up, thinking it's *mano a mano*, but he starts letting off with a pistol. Something tears through your shoulder. It hurts more than the buckshot. For the first time, your eyes meet his, and you aim. You pull the trigger three times before the slide on your weapon pulls back, telling you that it's empty.

There are two holes in the left side of Will's chest. He's not shooting anymore. You fall to the floor. Your legs don't seem to work. You slide your pistol under a couch. Then comes the pattering of the FDNY. The police will follow—as soon as you get patched up, as soon as they pronounce him dead, as soon as you know for sure that it's all over.

Everything goes black.

The next eighteen hours go by without you knowing it. You undergo surgery to have several ball bearings removed. A hollow point broke your clavicle but came out through your shoulder at an odd angle. There may be nerve damage and you will definitely need physical therapy.

On the other side of the bloodbath, you learn that there were others who survived. None of them are saying that you fired a single shot. The gun they match to Will has all the makings of self-defense. It's not that his crew isn't carrying a grudge. They just want to handle this on the street.

Detectives A and B, with whom you are more than familiar from your last run-in, are forced to accept your story about coming there on Chief's behalf, about arriving back in town to try and broker a truce. But Chief never showed for the meet. Will blamed you. The van exploded while you were inside. You heard gunshots. Will assumed you'd set him up. You grabbed a gun off a table and defended yourself. You try to keep the details as close to what you think science and circumstance can support. With no talking witnesses, they can't stick you with much.

No one can place you in Dumbo. As far as residents of the surrounding buildings were concerned, a bunch of black guys just started shooting at each other. The neighbors all hit the deck when they heard the guns, worried about catching strays. By the time they were done pissing in their pants and tried to call the cops, you and the van were gone and the only thing the crime scene needed was a hose and a meat wagon.

You sweeten your walking papers with info on all the stashes you know about. You give them the addresses for Will's house and Chief's mother's apartment, and all the details Chief told you about the operation. They put out feelers and they find enough drugs and guns to make the front page of the next morning's *Daily News*. For them, it's the stuff of commendations and interviews on NY1, a chance for their work to matter, a chance to get their Fed applications moved higher up on the pile. As a reward, they give you a ride to your rooming house when you're finally released from the hospital.

Brooklyn Hospital gives you a thirty-day prescription for Percocet and a referral for a physical therapist in Atlanta. In forty-eight hours you're back on the road.

You sell the CRX to a used car place three blocks from your house. You take 500 for it. The money pays for your plane ticket. You'll get a new ride to go with your new life. You don't want to drive all the way back. You want to pop some pills and spend a couple of hours in Never-Never Land.

"So where you from?" the country boy in front of you in line asks.

You can tell that he's never been up north. You can tell that he's probably never spent any real time outside of his hometown. The pace all around him is faster than anything he's ever known.

"Brooklyn," you say.

"That's where Fabolous from, right?"

You nod, then ask, "Where you from?"

"Athens," he says. You should've put money on it. Athens is barely two hours away.

The registrar checks your account balance and approves your class schedule. You're taking a full load. You already have books and you've been doing the readings. You eat lunch in a school cafeteria with the ambience of a prison mess hall. One week in and there's nothing better than getting back to higher learning and higher learning alone.

"I missed you, Daddy," Jenny says, as she runs her fingers along the outline of the bandage across your shoulder.

"I missed you too."

When she kisses you, her thighs feel like silk against your own. She smells like peaches.

"I wanna give you something," she says. After the session you two have just had, you don't think she could give you any more. But as she straddles you once again, you're willing to accept that you could be wrong. Her hands pull your eyelids shut.

"What you got for me?"

"Will said to tell you goodbye."

Your eyes pop open as soon as she removes her hand. You see the barrel of the .25 just as it explodes. One bullet in one brain.

The End.

All that dough and you'll never get your diploma. You thought it was going to be Star. But he's as gone as last week's discount sale. Live through one round with death and he comes back bigger and stronger in round two.

To be honest, you can't say that this is a real surprise. Living by the sword comes back to you.

Living by the gun only accelerates the process. You were never getting out. You were never going free. Time runs out for those who waste. Karma's a bitch for those who don't respect her power.

As you hover above your own body, you watch the bitch slip her clothes on far faster than it took for you to get them off. The light shining over you is an express train to the next life. Chief didn't have it all wrong. You didn't have it all right. But you'll get another chance. We all get another chance.

Also from **AKASHIC BOOKS**

GOT a debut novel by D
174 pages, trade paperback original, $13.95
*The first title from Kenji Jasper's imprint, The Armory

"There's a new player stepping into the street-lit spotlight, and he's one to watch."
—*Library Journal* (starred review)

"Packed with a rare combination of drama and class, *Got* has all the elements of an urban classic in the vein of *Carlito's Way* and *Bodega Dreams*. Let the poseurs beware: In his first time out, D doesn't just raise the bar on street lit, he broke the damn thing!"
—Black Artemis, author of *Picture Me Rollin'*

BROOKLYN NOIR
edited by Tim McLoughlin
350 pages, trade paperback original, $15.95
*Winner of Shamus, Anthony, and Robert L. Fish Memorial awards; finalist for an Edgar Award and a Pushcart Prize

Brand new stories by: Pete Hamill, Kenji Jasper, Arthur Nersesian, Ken Bruen, Sidney Offit, Maggie Estep, Nelson George, Chris Niles, Ellen Miller, and others.

"An excellent collection of Brooklyn stories that I urge everyone to read."
—Marty Markowitz, Brooklyn Borough President

D.C. NOIR
edited by George Pelecanos
282 pages, trade paperback original, $14.95

Brand new stories by: Laura Lippman, Kenji Jasper, Norman Kelley, Ruben Castaneda, Jennifer Howard, and others.

"[*D.C. Noir*] offers a startling glimpse into the cityscape's darkest corners . . . [with] solid writing, palpable tension and surprise endings."
—*Washington Post Book World*